✔ **KU-799-096**

ASTONISHING ACCLAIM FOR
BRIAR ROSE
BY JANE YOLEN

A 1992 Nebula Nominee

"One of [the Fairy Tales series'] most ambitious efforts, and only a writer as good as Yolen could bring it off. Yolen takes the story of Briar Rose (commonly known as Sleeping Beauty) and links it to the Holocaust—a far-from-obvious connection that she makes perfectly convincing. . . . She handles a difficult subject with finesse in a book that should be required reading for anyone who is tempted to dismiss fantasy as a frivolous genre."

—*Publishers Weekly*

"Both heartbreaking and heartwarming, Yolen's novel is a compelling reminder of the Holocaust as well as a contemporary tale of secrets and romance."

—*Booklist*

"The words leap off the page, creating such vivid pictures, that this reader, who has read volumes about the Holocaust, still found herself gasping aloud at times. . . . *Briar Rose* is an incredibly moving story about victims and about survivors. And though it is a fairy tale, not everyone lives happily ever after. . . . There is no record of a woman ever surviving Chelmno: thus, as fiction writers, we must create their stories and give voice to their tragedies. Jane Yolen has done just that, and she has done a magnificent job."

—Leslea Newman,
Bay Windows

"Her hands-down best ... Jane Yolen has long been a writer expert at the beautifully-turned phrase, and masterful in gently conveying a character's pain, but never has she seemed so committed to a piece of fiction, not even the awards-winning *The Devil's Arithmetic*."

—*Locus*

"Surpassing feeling and resonance ... Yolen has viewed 'Sleeping Beauty' as an allegory of history and made it fit events far more recent than anyone else might have dreamed possible. In the process, she has given the fairy tale a life far more real, more poignant, than anything the Disney wizards could possibly achieve."

—*Analog*

"A compact knockout of a novel ... Recommended."

—*Feminist Bookstore News*

"Showcases Yolen's skill at transforming the real world into a realm of fantasy."

—*Library Journal*

"A brilliant and very emotionally powerful novel you'll have to read in a single setting."

—*Science Fiction Chronicle*

"Terri Windling's Fairy Tale series shows over and over again that difficult truths can sometimes only be told through the medium of fantasy and fairy tales. In *Briar Rose* Jane Yolen tells one of the darkest tales of the twentieth century in spare, lyric prose, showing us obliquely a truth too terrifying to be faced directly, giving us a beautiful tale of darkness and redemption."

—Lisa Goldstein,
author of *The Red Magician*

"Jane Yolen has combined the magic of fairy-tale with the nightmare of history to produce an astonishing and astonishingly beautiful novel."

—Jay Neugeboren,
author of *The Stolen Jew*

"*Briar Rose* is one of those rare books that you don't so much read as experience. I first read the manuscript the way one downs a shot of good whisky, and the flavors stayed on my tongue a long time and sent a warm glow all through me."

—Steven Brust,
author of *The Phoenix Guards*

"Lyric and powerful ... *Briar Rose* takes the real world, full of genocidal butchers and bigoted peasants, and allows an air of magic to illuminate and give transcendence to the nightmare."

—*The New York Review of SF*

THE FAIRY TALE SERIES
EDITED BY TERRI WINDLING

OTHER TOR BOOKS BY JANE YOLEN

NOVELS:

EDITED BY JANE YOLEN:

BRIAR ROSE

Jane Yolen, P.J.F.

THE FAIRY TALE SERIES
CREATED BY TERRI WINDLING

TOR
fantasy

A TOM DOHERTY ASSOCIATES BOOK
NEW YORK

First published 1992 by Tom Doherty Associates Inc. New York

This edition published 1994 by Pan Books Limited
a division of Pan Macmillan Publishers Limited
Cavaye Place London SW10 9PG
and Basingstoke

Associated companies throughout the world

ISBN 0 330 33447 6

Introduction copyright © 1992 by Terri Windling
Copyright © 1992 by Jane Yolen

The right of Jane Yolen to be identified as the
author of this work has been asserted by her in accordance
with the Copyright, Designs and Patents Act 1988.

All rights reserved. No reproduction, copy or transmission
of this publication may be made without written permission.
No paragraph of this publication may be reproduced, copied or
transmitted save with written permission or in accordance with
the provisions of the Copyright Act 1956 (as amended). Any
person who does any unauthorised act in relation to
this publication may be liable to criminal prosecution
and civil claims for damages.

1 3 5 7 9 8 6 4 2

A CIP catalogue record for this book is available from
the British Library

Printed and bound in Great Britain by
Cox & Wyman Ltd, Reading, Berkshire

This book is sold subject to the condition that it shall not,
by way of trade or otherwise, be lent, re-sold, hired out,
or otherwise circulated without the publisher's prior consent
in any form of binding or cover other than that in which
it is published and without a similar condition including this
condition being imposed on the subsequent purchaser

For Charles and Maryann de Lint
and Susan Shwartz—just because
With special thanks to Barbara Diamond Goldin, Staszek
Radosh, Linda Mannheim, Betsy Pucci, Peter Gherlone,
Mary Teifke, Alissa Gehan, Susan Landau, and Scott
Scanlon for their research help. Any mistakes made in the
presentation of that material are mine alone.

"... (B)oth the oral and the literary forms of the fairy tale are grounded in history: they emanate from specific struggles to humanize bestial and barbaric forces, which have terrorized our minds and communities in concrete ways, threatening to destroy free will and human compassion. The fairy tale sets out to conquer this concrete terror through metaphors."

—*Jack Zipes*, Spells of Enchantment

BRIAR
ROSE

INTRODUCTION

FAIRY TALES

There is no satisfactory equivalent to the German word *märchen*, tales of magic and wonder such as those collected by the Brothers Grimm: *Rapunzel, Hansel & Gretel, Rumpelstiltskin, The Six Swans*, and other such familiar stories. We call them fairy tales, although none of the above stories actually contains a creature called a "fairy." They do contain those ingredients most familiar to us in fairy tales: magic and enchantment, spells and curses, witches and trolls, and protagonists ·who defeat overwhelming odds to triumph over evil. J. R. R. Tolkien, in his classic essay "On Fairy-Stories," offers the definition that these are not in particular tales about fairies or elves, but rather of the land of Faerie: "the Perilous Realm itself, and the air that blows in the country. I will not attempt to define that directly," he goes on, "for it cannot be done. Faerie cannot be caught in a net of words; for it is one of its qualities to be indescribable, though not imperceptible."

Fairy tales were originally created for an adult audience. The tales collected in the German countryside and set to paper by the Brothers Grimm (wherein a queen orders her stepdaughter, Snow·White, killed and her heart served "boiled and salted for my dinner") were published for an adult readership and were popular, in the age of Goethe and Schiller, among the German Romantic poets. Charles Perrault's spare and moralistic tales (such as Little Red Riding Hood who, in the original Perrault telling, gets eaten by the wolf in the end for having the ill sense to talk to strangers in the wood) were written for the court of Louis XIV; Madame d'Aulnoy (author of *The White Cat*) and Madame Leprince de Beaumont (author of *Beauty and the Beast*) also wrote for the French aristocracy. In England, fairy stories and heroic legends were popularized through Malory's Arthur, Shakespeare's Puck and Ariel, and Spenser's Faerie Queene.

With the Age of Enlightenment and the growing emphasis on rational and scientific modes of thought, along with the rise in fashion of novels of social realism in the nineteenth century, literary fantasy went out of vogue and those stories of magic, enchantment, heroic quests, and courtly romance that form a cultural heritage thousands of years old, dating back to the oldest written epics and further still to tales spoken around the hearth-fire, came to be seen as fit only for children, relegated to the nursery like, Professor Tolkien points out, "shabby or old fashioned furniture . . . primarily because the adults do not want it, and do not mind if it is misused."

And misused the stories have been, in some cases altered to make them suitable for Victorian children, so greatly that the original tales were all but forgotten. Andrew Lang's *Tam Lin*, printed in the colored Fairy Books series, tells the story of little Janet whose playmate is stolen away by the fairy folk—ignoring the original, darker tale of seduction and human sacrifice to the Lord of Hell, as the heroine, pregnant with Tam Lin's child, battles the Fairy Queen for her lover's life. Walt Disney's *Sleeping Beauty* bears only a little resemblance to Straparola's *Sleeping Beauty of the Wood*, published in Venice in the sixteenth century, in which the enchanted princess is impregnated as she sleeps, waking to find herself the mother of twins. The Little Golden Book version of the *Arabian Nights* resembles not at all the violent and sensual tales actually recounted by Scheherazade in *One Thousand and One Nights*, shocking nineteenth-century Europe when fully translated by Sir Richard Burton. ("*Not* for the young and innocent . . ." said the *Daily Mail*.)

The wealth of material from myth and folklore at the disposal of the story-teller (or modern fantasy novelist) has been described as a giant cauldron of soup into which each generation throws new bits of fancy and history, new imaginings, new ideas, to simmer along with the old. The story-teller is the cook who serves up the common ingredients in his or her own individual way, to suit the tastes of a new audience. Each generation has its cooks, its Hans Christian Andersen or Charles Perrault, spinning magical tales for those who will listen—even amid the Industrial Revolution of the nineteenth century or the technological revolution of our own. In the last century, George MacDonald, William Morris, Christina Rossetti, and Oscar Wilde, among others, turned their hands to fairy stories; at the turn of the century lavish fairy tale collections were produced, a showcase for the art of Arthur Rackham, Edmund Dulac, Kai Nielsen, the Robinson Brothers— published as children's books, yet often found gracing adult salons.

In the early part of the twentieth century Lord Dunsany, G. K. Chesterton, C. S. Lewis, T. H. White, J. R. R. Tolkien—to name but a few—created classic tales of fantasy; while more recently we've seen the growing popularity of books published under the category title "Adult Fantasy"—as well as works published in the literary mainstream that could easily go under that heading: John Barth's *Chimera*, John Gardner's *Grendel*, Joyce Carol Oates' *Bellefleur*, Sylvia Townsend Warner's *Kingdoms of Elfin*, Mark Halprin's *A Winter's Tale*, and the works of South American writers such as Gabriel García Márquez and Miguel Angel Asturias.

It is not surprising that modern readers or writers should occasionally turn to fairy tales. The fantasy story or novel differs from novels of social realism in that it is free to portray the world in bright, primary colors, a dream-world half remembered from the stories of childhood when all the world was bright and strange, a fiction unembarrassed to tackle the large themes of Good and Evil, Honor and Betrayal, Love and Hate. Susan Cooper, who won the Newbery Medal for her fantasy novel *The Grey King*, makes this comment about the desire to write fantasy: "In the *Poetics* Aristotle said, 'A likely impossibility is always preferable to an unconvincing possibility.' I think those of us who write fantasy are dedicated to making impossible things seem likely, making dreams seem real. We are somewhere between the Impressionist and abstract painters. Our writing is haunted by those parts of our experience which we do not understand, or even consciously remember. And if you, child or adult, are drawn to our work, your response comes from that same shadowy land."

All Adult Fantasy stories draw in a greater or lesser degree from traditional tales and legends. Some writers consciously acknowledge that material like J. R. R. Tolkien who used themes and imagery from the Icelandic Eddas and the German *Niebelungenlied* in *The Lord of the Rings* or Evangeline Walton who reworked the stories from the Welsh *Mabinogion* in *The Island of the Mighty*. Some narratives use the language and symbols of old tales to create new ones, such as the stories collected in Jane Yolen's *Tales of Wonder*, or Patricia McKillip's *The Forgotten Beasts of Eld*. And other writers, like Robin McKinley in *Beauty* or Angela Carter in *The Bloody Chamber* (and the movie *The Company of Wolves* derived from a story in that collection) base their stories directly on old tales, breathing new life into them, and presenting them to the modern reader.

The Fairy Tales series presents novels of the later sort— novels directly based on traditional fairy tales. Each novel in the series is based on a specific, often familiar, tale—yet each author is free to retell that story in his or her own way, showing the diverse uses a modern story-teller can make of traditional material. In the early novels of the Fairy Tale series, published by Ace Books, Steven Brust used a folk tale from his Hungarian heritage to mirror a contemporary story of artists and courage and the act of creation in *The Sun, the Moon, and the Stars*. In *Jack the Giant-Killer*, Charles de Lint created a faery world in the shadows of a modern Canadian city; as with the Latin American "magic realists," the fantasy in this novel tells us much about the real world and one young woman's confrontation with the secret places in her own heart. In *The Nightingale*, Kara Dalkey turned Hans Christian Andersen's classic story into a haunting historical novel set in ancient Japan, a tale of love and magic and poetry which evokes the life of the Japanese imperial court as deftly as did the diaries of the imperial court ladies, written so many centuries ago.

With the fourth volume, the Fairy Tale series moved to Tor Books. In *Snow White and Rose Red*, Patricia C. Wrede moved the Grimm fairy tale into an Elizabethan milieu, creating a charming and romantic novel set in the enchanted forest of an England that never was. And in *Tam Lin*, Pamela Dean transformed the Scots fairy tale and folk-ballad of that name into a novel of knowledge and danger set at a modern midwestern university.

The novel you hold in your hands, the sixth in the Fairy Tale Series, is by one of the most acclaimed makers of modern *marchen*, Jane Yolen. Yolen has taken the German tale *Briar Rose*, also known as *Sleeping Beauty in the Wood*, and turned it into a contemporary tale both dark and bright, both terrifying and inspiring. It is an honor to include this excellent novel by one of my all-time favorite writers in our ongoing Fairy Tale series.

We have more Fairy Tales in the works for you by some of the most talented writers working today, re-telling the world's most beloved tales in editions lovingly designed (by the award-winning Boston artist/illustrator Thomas Canty) as all good fairy tales should be.

I hope you enjoy them all.

—TERRI WINDLING

Editor, The Fairy Tale Series
Devon, England, and
Tucson, Arizona, 1992

HOME

But far above these as a source of myth, are the half-heard scraps of gossip, from parent to parent, neighbor to neighbor as they whisper across a fence. A hint, a carefully garbled disclosure, a silencing finger at the lip, and the tales, like rain clouds, gather. It could almost be said that a listening child has no need to read the tales. A keen ear and the power to dissemble—he must not seem to be listening—are all that is required.

—P.L. Travers: About the Sleeping Beauty

Everyone likes a fairy story because everyone wants things to come right in the end. And even though to tell a story is to tell some kind of untruth, one often suspects that what seems to be untruth is really a hidden truth.

—Ralph Harper: The Sleeping Beauty

CHAPTER

1

"*Gemma, tell your story again,*" Shana begged, putting her arms around her grandmother and breathing in that special smell of talcum and lemon that seemed to belong only to her.

"*Which one?*" Gemma asked, chopping the apples in the wooden bowl.

"*You know,*" Shana said.

"*Yes—you know,*" Sylvia added. Like her sister, she crowded close and let the talcum-lemon smell almost overwhelm her.

Baby Rebecca in the high chair banged her spoon against the cup. "Seepin Boot. Seepin Boot."

Shana made a face. Even when she had been little herself she'd never spoken in baby talk. Only full sentences; her mother swore to it.

"*Seepin Boot.*" Gemma smiled. "*All right.*"

The sisters nodded and stepped back a pace each, as if the story demanded their grandmother's face, not just her scent.

"*Once upon a time,*" Gemma began, the older two girls whispering the opening with her, "*which is all times and no times but not the very best of times, there was a castle.*

And in it lived a king who wanted nothing more in the world than a child.

" 'From your lips to God's ears,' the queen said each time the king talked of a baby. But the years went by and they had none.' "

"None, none, none," sang out Rebecca, banging her spoon on the cup with each word.

"Shut up!" Shana and Sylvia said in unison.

Gemma took the spoon and cup away and gave Rebecca a slice of apple instead. "Now one day, finally and at last and about time, the queen went to bed and gave birth to a baby girl with a crown of red hair." Gemma touched her own hair in which strands of white curled around the red like barbed wire. "The child's face was as beautiful as a wildflower and so the king named her ..."

"Briar Rose," Sylvia and Shana breathed.

"Briar Rose," repeated Rebecca, only not nearly so clearly, her mouth being quite full of apple.

CHAPTER

2

It was spring, or at least so the calendar said, but a soft snow had been falling all night, coating the Holyoke streets. The Lynx labored up the slippery hill, chugging instead of purring like the Mercedes they'd had to leave behind in the shop.

"I *told* Mother that Mercedes was a lemon, but she only laughed," Sylvia said, playing once again with her goldshrimp earring. She'd already worried the right one off and was at work on the left.

"And *I* told her Father would have done a damned sight better taking a mistress instead of a Mercedes for his midlife crisis. For one thing, they're cheaper!" Shana always had to get off the better lines.

The two of them smiled at each other, their quick tongues, dark hair, wide-set eyes, and high cheekbones marking them as twins, though actually they were eighteen months apart.

Becca, the youngest, smiled at them both, but she was not part of their magic circle and never had been. Guiding the sputtering little beige car up the last hill, she forced it through an attempted spin-out with a sure hand.

"Come on, Rocinante," she murmured. The car had already been very secondhand when she bought it and Rocinante was the only name that presented itself at the time. She never felt right about owning something that performed for her without giving it a name. "Come on, baby, up and over."

The Lynx managed to crest the hill and Becca turned it expertly to the right on Cabot Street, coasting to a stop in front of the three-story brick nursing home.

"Here we are," she said, as much to the car as to her sisters.

Sylvia and Shana got out quickly, volleying curses at the snow, and walked in briskly. They didn't even stop to stomp off the wet, clinging snow from their Ferragamo boots.

After locking all four doors of the car, Becca followed. At the last minute she lifted her face to the snow and tongued in some snowflakes. *Magic,* she thought. Even when she had to drive in it, snow had always held some kind of magic. Especially this year, with a drought forecast on every channel.

There was a musicale in progress in the Home's square entry hall. It was being led by a balding man with a banjo who urged everyone to sing along in a voice made breathless by his enthusiasm. About forty residents, in five fairly even lines of wheelchairs and straightbacked rockers, were trying to follow his lead. Except for Mrs. Hartshorn, off in the corner again, tying knots in her long, faded hair like a white Rastafarian. Even the nurses ignored her.

"Hello, Mrs. Hartshorn," Becca said companionably as she went by, not expecting any answer, and not getting any.

A ragged chorus of "Oh, Susannah" was straggling towards some kind of conclusion with at least two of the staff attempting harmony. Becca checked but didn't see her grandmother in the crowd. Since they'd been summoned because Gemma was failing rapidly, Becca only looked from habit. Some of the residents recognized her and Mr. Silvers waved. She blew him a kiss which he caught in an exaggerated mime, as a child might.

Shana was already stabbing away at the elevator button as if expecting that repeated jabs would bring it faster. And Sylvia was replacing her earrings and pulling the taupe sweater down over her flat stomach.

Becca didn't hurry. She knew it would be a while before the crotchety machine answered its summons, even longer before it would settle with a squeal onto the first floor.

When the door creaked open at last, two of the nursing staff pushed out.

"Why, hello, Becca," said one. "She was alert and asking for you this morning."

The other merely inclined her head. She was Mrs. Hartshorn's private-duty nurse.

Becca smiled at them both, an extra-broad grin to compensate for her sisters who hadn't even acknowledged the nurses' presence, as if white uniforms rendered them invisible. Then she crowded into the small elevator, elbow to elbow with Shana.

"Three," Becca prompted, doubting either of them remembered. They'd only visited twice in four years, living so far away, one in L.A., one in Houston.

"I know, I know," Shana said with an exaggerated sigh. "I *have* been here before."

"We both have," Sylvia added, now playing with the heavy gold chain around her neck, picking at the Hands of God as if she could pry them apart. "But it's so hard, Becca, I don't know how you manage, visiting every day."

"It's not *every* day," Becca whispered.

"I mean," Sylvia kept on as if Becca hadn't spoken, "if I lived here, I couldn't see her every day. Not in this place. Not the way she is now."

Becca smiled again, but closed her eyes because she was afraid that if she kept them open, they would see she was on the verge of tears. And then they'd start in on her again, about how at Gemma's age, with the arthritis and diabetes, it was just as well she didn't know anything, couldn't suffer, as though the body felt no pain if the mind wandered in the past. Gemma wasn't *that* old and she was *far* from senile, Becca thought fiercely, the anger at last fighting back the tears.

She was about to remark aloud on it when the elevator stopped and the door opened onto the nurse's station. No one was there, but an open notebook and scattered papers on the countertop were evidence of recent activity.

"I *hate* the smell of these places," Sylvia said, her hands now on her hair, nervously smoothing the sides, checking the black velvet bow. "I don't know how the people here stand it."

"Mostly they *lie* in it," Shana said. "Old houses and old people smell and I don't plan to live in the one or be the other."

"Think of the alternative," Becca muttered, angry with herself for rising to Shana's bait. Apart, her sisters were strong, competent women, Shana in real estate and Sylvia a social worker. But together they became bickering children. Becca knew this, had spent days preparing herself for their visit. Yet again, like every other time they came back home, the quarreling had started. She bit her lip and silently led the way down the hall. Only Mrs. Benton was still in her room, crying softly to herself. Becca couldn't think of a time when she visited that Mrs. Benton wasn't crying, calling out for her mother. The rest of Third West were downstairs finishing "Oh, Susannah" and probably starting on "You Are My Sunshine," but Mrs. Benton was sobbing like a heartbroken child.

Becca turned sharply into room 310 and looked around at the neat, spare furnishings. They'd been lucky to get this room because Gemma loved sunlight and it was an unusually sunny corner room. Today, though, with the snow falling outside, the room was gray and cold.

"Hello, Gemma," Becca said brightly to the old woman propped up in the bed. The bearclaws quilt was tucked in so tightly around her, it was almost possible to ignore the fact that she had on a posie restraint, tying her to the bedsides. The television was crooning a game show. Sylvia snapped it off in passing.

Shana went over and kissed her grandmother on the cheek, dry little kisses that barely touched the skin yet still left marks where they landed because the old woman's skin was so brittle. Sylvia waited her turn and then did the same, missing the cheek by a hair's breadth. There were tears shimmering in her eyes. She lowered the side of the bed and kissed her again.

Having done their duty, Shana and Sylvia straightened up and Sylvia went to stare out the window at the snow. Shana moved to the foot of the bed and set her Vuitton tote softly on top of the quilt.

Sitting on the edge of the bed, Becca took Gemma's hand in hers. It felt boneless, as though whoever had once resided in the skin had moved, gone.

"Left no forwarding address," Shana whispered, as if reading Becca's thoughts.

"Gemma? Gemma, it's me, Becca," Becca said breathily. "I've brought Syl and Shana to see you. We love you."

"We love you," they chorused dutifully.

For a long moment there was no response at all and Becca wondered if Shana had been right and there was truly no one home. Then, as if slowly returning from a far journey, Gemma filled her skin again, breathed a shuddering sigh, and opened her eyes. They were the faded blue of a late winter sky.

Becca squeezed her grandmother's hand carefully, aware how fragile a thing it was she held. "Gemma . . ." she began again.

"Once upon a time," Gemma said, her voice like a child's, high and whispery. "Which is all times and no times but not . . ." She stopped, drew in a little breath that nonetheless seemed to fill her up again, ". . . the best of times." Her breath was as pale as her skin and smelled like old potpourri, musty and sweet.

"Oh God," Sylvia said, her voice tight, "not *that* again."

She didn't leave the window and stared even more intently at the snow, as if fascinated by it, but her shoulders were shaking and Becca hoped she wasn't going to cry. Sylvia was a noisy weeper, as if she were trying to bring everyone in on her grief, and Gemma always became agitated when someone near her cried.

"Once upon a time there was a castle," Gemma said. She stopped.

"What castle?" prompted Becca.

"We all know *what* castle, Becca. Leave it!" Picking off an invisible hair from her cream-colored blazer, Shana hissed, "Don't make it any worse than it is."

Becca opened her mouth to argue, but the old woman had fallen back to sleep.

They waited about twenty minutes, but she didn't rouse again.

"That's it, then," Sylvia said, consulting a thin gold watch and turning briskly from the window. "Time to go." Her eyes were red and there was a single thin mascara line down her right cheek.

"She may come 'round again," Becca said, almost pleading. "She often does. And you've both come so far to see her. You may not get another . . . another . . . chance. Not before she . . ." She couldn't bring herself to finish the sentence, as if *death* were too final a punctuation. "Let's not go already."

"*Already?* It's three o'clock and still snowing and we'll have to fight traffic soon." Sylvia held up her hand, the one with the watch, as if that added force to her argument. She was clearly uncomfortable, almost afraid.

"Traffic?"

"Oh, right, I forgot we're back in the boonies. No L.A. traffic here, then. Or Houston." She looked meaningfully at Shana.

Shana leaned over and put her arm around Becca. "Listen, we both know it's hardest on you and we're trying to make it easier, at least for today. You're the one who does all the visiting after all."

"But Mama and Daddy . . ." Becca said loyally.

"*We* know who does the most visiting," Shana said. "*Everyone* knows. So you don't have to try and share *everything*." She looked over at Sylvia and shook her head, as if to warn her off.

"But Bec," Sylvia said, ignoring the warnings and tapping her own head ominously.

"She is *not* crazy," Becca said, her voice rising to the old whine she couldn't help when she was around her sisters too long.

"Not, not crazy. Not at all. Only she thinks—she *believes*—she once lived in a castle! The true *Belle au Bois Dormant*." Sylvia's accent was impeccable. She'd studied at the Sorbonne her junior year in college. "The Sleeping Beauty in the Wood. A goddamned fairy tale princess, Becca. With a Yiddish accent. If *she's* not crazy believing it—you are. Grow up, Becca. Shana and I have."

"It's not that," Becca said, trying to explain. "I mean, it's not that I believe it. Or even that she does. It's like the story is . . . like a metaphor. . . ."

Sylvia snorted, the familiar bickering overcoming what lingering grief she had felt. "A *meddlefur*," she said, using the old baby word the family favored. "Thank goodness you decided against graduate school and stuck with that silly underground newspaper you work for."

"It's not *underground*; it's *alternative* and . . ."

"What's the difference," Sylvia said, turning away. "The left wing is the left wing whether it's above or below the dirt."

"You don't *want* to understand," Becca said, tears spilling down her cheeks and making her feel years younger than twenty-three, making her wonder why only her sisters could start her crying.

"Once upon a time . . ." Gemma's voice interrupted them. All three turned to stare at her. The old woman's eyes remained firmly closed.

"Now you've done it," Sylvia hissed. "She's awake again. She'll tell that beastly story."

"Which is all times and no times but not the very best of times," the whispery voice continued, "there was a castle. And in it lived a king who wanted nothing more in the world but a child." Her voice seemed to be gathering strength from the telling and she moved swiftly through the well-worn opening. "Now one day, finally and at last and about time, the queen went to bed and gave birth to a baby girl with a crown of red hair." Gemma tried to reach up to touch her own hair, but the posie kept her from moving and she hesitated as if the story had been—somehow—set awry. Then, drawing in another whispery breath, she went on. "The child's face was as beautiful as a wildflower and so the king named her . . ." She stopped.

"Briar Rose," the three sisters chorused, as quickly as if they were youngsters again enjoying the story though, by their faces, two at least were angry and one—as red-haired as the princess in the tale—was in tears.

As if their antiphonal response was all the assurance she needed, the old woman fell asleep again. Looking conspiratorially at one another, Sylvia and Shana slipped away from the bed and headed for the door.

"Bec—" Shana called from the doorway.

Becca shook her head and didn't move. She meant by that headshake that she would stay, that she forgave them their desertion. And she did. It was an awful, urine-smelling place and there was a terrible sense of sadness and defeat underlying it, despite the silver tea service from which the residents drank their ten o'clock tea and the four o'clock Happy Hour and the cheery crafts room and the desperate strains of "Clementine" and "Down by the Old Mill Stream" drifting up the elevator shaft. She understood her sisters entirely and loved them, even though she often hated the things they said. It was why she came to the nursing home every afternoon after work at the newspaper and stayed with Gemma three and four hours each weekend, afraid that Gemma might become a Mrs. Hartshorn who never had visitors and made macrame of her hair. Or a Mrs. Benton who never stopped crying for a mother who never came. Or a Mrs. Gedowski on Two West who sat in the hall cursing, in graphic detail that even rap singers would have envied.

They left and Becca sat listening to their footsteps fade down the hall. She could hear the bustle of the Home outside the door: the elevator clanking and wheezing its way down to the first floor, a telephone ringing twice at the nurse's station before being answered by a weary voice. A cart rattled by, accompanied by the *slip-slap* of a nurse's cushioned shoes. The television announcer's cheery banter almost covered the sound of Mrs. Benton's weeping.

Standing, Becca went to the door, closed it, then returned to her grandmother's bed. This time when she picked up Gemma's hand, there was a desperate strength in it.

"Rebecca?" Gemma's whispery voice seemed stronger. "Rebecca!"

"Here I am, Gemma."

The old woman opened her eyes. "*I* was the princess in the castle in the sleeping woods. And there came a great dark mist and we all fell asleep. But the prince kissed me awake. Only me."

"Yes, Gemma," Becca replied, soothingly.

The old woman struggled against the restraints, trying to sit up. At last she stopped struggling and fell back helplessly. "*I was the princess!*" she cried again. "In the castle. The prince kissed me."

"Yes, Gemma."

"That castle is yours. It is all I have to leave you. You must find it. The castle in the sleeping woods. Promise me." She tried again to sit up, despite the posie, her face now spotty with agitation.

"I promise, Gemma."

"Promise me you will find the castle. Promise me you

will find the prince. Promise me you will find the. maker of the spells."

"I said I promise, Gemma." Becca couldn't believe the strength in her grandmother's hand.

"Swear it."

"I swear, Gemma."

"On my grave, swear it."

"You're not *dead*, Gemma." She hated saying the word. As if saying it made it real.

"Swear it."

"I swear. On . . . on your grave, Gemma."

The spottiness seemed to fade from the old woman's face and she lay back quietly, eyes closed again, whispering something that Becca, even straining, could not hear.

Becca leaned over, putting her ear as close to the old woman's mouth as she dared, fearing she might suffocate Gemma by accident. Finally she could make out the words.

"I am Briar Rose," Gemma was repeating. "I am Briar Rose."

CHAPTER

3

"It's almost bedtime," Gemma said.

"You promised I could stay up because I'm ten," Sylvia said. "And I could have a story."

"But not Sleeping Beauty," Shana begged. "A new one."

"I want Sleeping Beauty," Becca said. "It's my favorite." Favorite was her latest and most special word.

"Sleeping Beauty for Becca, and then she goes to bed. Then another story for you two old ladies." Gemma smiled, but Shana and Sylvia left the room.

"We'll be back when Sleeping Beauty is over!" Shana called from the other room.

"And not before," Sylvia added.

But the story was only barely begun when they crept to the door's edge and listened.

Gemma was saying: ". . . so the king said it was time for a party."

"A big party?" asked Becca, already knowing the answer.

"A terrifically big party. With cake and ice cream and golden plates. And not to mention invitations sent to all the good fairies in the kingdom."

"But not the bad fairy."

Gemma pulled the child closer to her. "Not the bad fairy. Not the one in black with big black boots and silver eagles on her hat."

"But she came."

"She came, that angel of death. She came to the party and she said 'I curse you, Briar Rose. I curse you and your father the king and your mother the queen and all your uncles and cousins and aunts. And all the people in your village. And all the people who bear your name.' " Gemma shook herself all over and Becca put her hand on her grandmother's arm.

"It will be all right, Gemma. You'll see. The curse doesn't work."

Gemma gave her another hug and continued the story.

CHAPTER

4

The funeral was a small affair, only a couple dozen people at the synagogue. Gemma had been a private person and there wasn't much in the way of family. The rabbi had spoken about someone who had only vaguely resembled Gemma; Becca had had to keep bringing her mind back to the present and away from the stories Gemma used to tell. When the cantor began singing with a great deal of vibrato and at least a quarter tone flat, she gave up and retreated to the castle of her grandmother's favorite tale.

There were even fewer people at the cemetery off King Street. Trucks rumbled by as the rabbi said the final prayers, obscuring his words. Becca's soft snufflings were lost in the screech of tires as a teenager took off out of a driveway somewhere down the road, then honked his horn at a panicked squirrel.

Wrapped in a calf-length black mink coat, Sylvia shivered and spoke to her husband in a voice that carried. "April tenth and winter still. Why couldn't she have died in Florida, like your father?" She meant it as a whisper, as a bit of humor to buoy her own flagging spirits, but it was loud enough to cut across the rabbi's last words to the family. Becca looked at her sharply, the little wind bring-

ing tears to both their eyes. Embarrassed, Sylvia bit her lip
and looked down. When Becca turned her attention back
to the rabbi, he was done and, with an overturned shovel,
was shifting a little dirt into the open grave.

"Good-bye, Gemma," Becca whispered as the dirt pat-
tered down. She waited her turn to throw a handful in, first
lifting the earth to her nose. Sniffing it carefully, as if to
be sure the ground Gemma was to lie in had the proper
smell, she sighed. Then she knelt, drew in a breath so deep
it made her chest ache, and let the dirt tumble slowly out
of her palm.

"I promise, Gemma," she said under her breath. "I
swear." When she stood again, her father threaded his arm
through hers, holding her tightly as if afraid he was going
to lose her into the grave as well. They walked back to the
limo arm in arm, and she hadn't the heart to pry his fingers away, though she was sure he was leaving bruises.

More people came to the house than had attended the ser-
vices because most of their neighbors—men and women
who had known Gemma for over forty years—were Polish
and Catholic and made uncomfortable by the idea of going
into a synagogue, as if the church still forbade it. The
dining-room table groaned with their funeral offerings:
kielbasa, *galumpkis*, salads heavy with mayonnaise, lumpy
pies.

The house smelled overwhelmingly like spring, the
scents of all the bouquets overpowering even the smell of
the food. None of their neighbors believed that flowers
were inappropriate for a Jewish funeral, though Becca had
tried to tell them. Each time the front door opened, or the
back, letting in a new mourner, a fresh breeze stirred the
blossoms. Becca was sick with the smell.

Sylvia went upstairs to fix her hair one more time in
front of the mirror in her old bedroom. The downstairs
mirrors were all draped with cloth, not because the Berlins
were religious enough to follow conservative funeral customs, but because the rabbi—who was paying his

respects—would care. The draped mirrors had annoyed
Sylvia so much, she stomped up the stairs, dropping mud
from her boots and dumping her mink on the bed with an
angry shrug. Brushing off the silk shirt to rid it of hairs
only she could see, she stared critically at her reflection.

Her husband Mike smiled over her shoulder. "You look
fine, babe," he said.

"Fine isn't good enough." But she smiled back at him
via the mirror, as if to assure him it was.

When they went out into the hall, they met Shana and
her husband. Shana's cheeks had little bright spots on
them, a clear indication that she and Howie had had another argument.

"Where's Becca?" Sylvia asked.

"Downstairs. Serving coffee, no doubt. Dividing lumpy
pies. Entertaining Gemma's friends. What else?" Shana
answered, her fight with Howie making her sharper than
she meant.

The men's eyes met above their wives' heads. Howie
looked down first.

Becca was—in fact—cutting the pies and setting them out
on the good china, a fork with each plate. She felt her
hands needed something to do, unlike her mind, which she
kept busy with a complicated list of things still to be done,
a comforting mnemonic more soothing than a mantra. But
her hands kept shaking whenever they weren't working at
something. She knew it was a simple reaction to the emotion of the day, but she always had such physical reac-
tions: able to function in the immediate emergency, falling
apart afterwards. Just like her grandmother. It was a family
joke.

The Bukowskis, in loud unmodulated voices, were talking about Gemma in the TV room, their hands describing
circles that had nothing to do with the subject. And a small
knot of children—Shana's two girls and Sylvia's little boy
and the Berkowitz twins—were playing tag on the stairs.
Becca knew that she should go and deal with their noise

because she could see it was beginning to bother her mother, who sat swollen-eyed on the piano bench, surrounded by chatting neighbors. But Becca couldn't move, except to cut pies to stop the shaking in her hands.

On their way down the stairs, Sylvia and Shana dealt swiftly and professionally with the children, a kind of kangaroo court of mothers, sending them outside, even without their coats. Becca smiled. At any other time her sisters would have erred on the side of caution, loading up the children with sweaters and jackets. She took it as a sign that they were more moved by Gemma's death than either one would admit out loud.

"I could use some help," she called, a kind of peace offering. But they veered off into the family room and Becca felt that she couldn't intrude any further into their grief. Instead she began to cut a peach pie with a kind of frantic ferocity that looked a great deal like unspoken anger. Becca considered it part of her day's endless sorrow.

She thought of Gemma lying in the bed, eyes closed, whispering "I am Briar Rose."

Sleeping Beauty. How could she think of that? Gemma's fine hair had escaped its careful braiding and fanned out against the pillow. Not a bit of the red still showed. Her skin, like old parchment on a bone stretcher, had been maplike; the careful traceries of her age showing where and how she had lived. Except that none of them knew *where* she had lived as a child. Only that she had come to America before the Second World War.

"Maybe, Daddy, maybe she really *did* live in a castle somewhere in Europe. Like the Rothschilds, you know."

Her father, a handsome, balding man, his face still firm under the chin and his moustache a white parenthesis around his mouth, smiled and shook his head. "No castle, sweetheart. That's just one of Gemma's stories."

"She seemed awful certain of it."

"Nothing about your grandmother was certain," he said. "Not her date of birth, not her country of origin—not even her name."

"Gemma," Becca said automatically.

"That was because Shana couldn't say *Grandma*."

Becca looked down and cut another slice of pie, a thin slice, too small to be of interest to anyone but a dieter. "I knew that. I meant Dawna. Dawna Prinz. At least that's what I put down on that family tree we had to do in fourth grade. I remember because I almost had to do the whole thing over because I spelled it wrong till Mama found some white-out." She looked around for something else to cut.

Her father took the knife from her and set it carefully on a plate, as carefully as he placed his surgical instruments when he was finished with them.

"Dawna was the name she chose to be called," he said quietly. "But in the old country, she had another name— I'm sure."

"What was it?"

"How should I know?" Dr. Berlin shrugged broadly. "I was only her son-in-law. For almost thirty years. I was lucky she told me her daughter's name when we met. A great woman for secrets, your grandmother." He laughed and Becca tried to feel shocked that he could act like that today, of all days. Then, drawn into his laugh at last, as she always was, she let herself enjoy it.

Picking up several of the plates, she began circulating around the room, exchanging pieces of pie for murmurs of sympathy. Little pockets of laughter seemed to fade as she approached. When her hands were empty, she went back to get more pies.

By the time the neighbors left and only family remained, Becca was empty of tears. She sat at the kitchen table, eyes closed, listening. Her mother and father seemed almost happy, washing and drying the good china by hand and talking over the things people had said to them. From the living room came the sounds of CNN blaring the business news. She knew Shana and Sylvia and their husbands were collapsed in front of the television.

"Aunt Becca, tell us a story."

She opened her eyes. It was Benjamin, his fair hair cut in low bangs. He looked so much like his father, she smiled. Imagine trying to tell Mike a story! But Shana's two little girls were right by his side, their eyes pleading. "All right. But only one. What should I tell?"

"Seepin Boot," whispered Sarah. Benjamin punched her arm.

"Not *that* one. That's Gemma's!"

"I'd like to tell that one," Becca said. "*Because* it's Gemma's."

"Won't she be mad?" asked Susan.

"Don't be silly," Benjamin said. "She's dead."

"Well, ghosts could get mad," Susan countered.

"Jews don't *believe* in ghosts," Benjamin stated with great authority. Then he looked over at Becca. "Do we?"

She shook her head, not because she didn't believe in ghosts, but because the conversation was obviously frightening Sarah, who leaned against her.

"Even if Gemma were a ghost," Becca said, "she'd be a loving ghost. And she would want me to tell Sleeping Beauty to you. In fact the very last thing she talked to me about was Briar Rose."

The shadow across Sarah's face lightened and she smiled. "Once upon a time . . ." she prompted and Becca, smiling back, began.

When the children were finally in bed, the adults gathered in the dining room.

"Gemma left a regular will," Dr. Berlin said. "That's what comes of having lawyers in the family." He nodded at Mike. "But Gemma had a box of things which your mother and I thought we should open tonight, now that we are all together."

"What's in it, Daddy?" Sylvia asked, pulling the black bow out of her hair and running her fingernails lightly across the back of her neck.

"We don't know. It was Gemma's secret. Mama didn't

even know about it until we unpacked the dresser yesterday, the one in the nursing home. It's—"

Mrs. Berlin interrupted, "It's full of . . . well . . . stuff."
She spoke so softly, Becca had to lean forward to hear.

Dr. Berlin patted his wife's hand twice, then stood and
went into the kitchen, returning with a wooden box with a
carved rose and briar on top.

"Not another damned rose," Howie said. "Gemma was
a textbook case of obsessive-compulsive."

"What do you know about such things?" Sylvia
snapped. "You're an orthodontist."

"Medical is medical," Shana answered.

"Is not," Sylvia said.

"Is."

"Is not."

Mike began to laugh nervously and Dr. Berlin held up
his hand.

Shana and Sylvia stopped their argument at once. In the
sudden silence Becca could hear her mother's ragged
breathing, just as she had all during her sisters' quarrel-
some adolescences.

"Can we see what's in the box, Mama?" Becca asked,
a kind of peace offering.

"We'll let Mama open it," Dr. Berlin said.

Slowly Mrs. Berlin raised the lid and they stared down
into a rat's nest of photos and papers. Then she took out
the pieces of paper one at a time, setting them carefully on
the dining room table until the table seemed patchworked.

"Look at this photo!" Sylvia called. "Is it Gemma?"

"And these clippings," Shana said, tapping one of the
yellowed papers with a bright red nail.

"Let's start at one end together," suggested Dr. Berlin,
picking up a photograph and turning it over. "Evie and me,
1945," he read aloud. He passed the photograph around. It
was a black-and-white picture of a woman in an ill-fitting
cotton dress holding a child with blonde pigtails and big
eyes.

"*Is* that you, Mama?" Becca asked, pointing to the child.

Her father laughed. "Of course. Who could miss those eyes."

"What a ghastly dress," Sylvia said. "Like flour sacking."

"It was the times," Mrs. Berlin murmured. "But I've never seen that picture before."

Becca picked up the next paper. "It's some sort of entry form," she said. "Into America." She looked slowly around the table. "For a Gitl Mandlestein."

"Gitl?" Shana asked.

"Maybe that was Gemma's real name," Howie said.

"No one I knew ever called her Gitl," Mrs. Berlin said. "But then I knew no one from the old country. I thought her name was Genevieve."

"You didn't know your own mother's *real* name?" Mike was amazed.

"I thought I was named Eve because of her being Genevieve," Mrs. Berlin said. "And then she took Dawna as a nickname so we'd be Dawn and Eve. She joked about it."

"And *I* always thought she took Dawna from the story," Sylvia said.

"What story?" Shana was clearly puzzled.

"Briar Rose, of course. You know—the princess Aurora. Dawn."

"That's too deep for me," Howie said.

"*Everything's* too . . ." Sylvia started.

"Syl!" The warning from Dr. Berlin was enough. He picked up another photograph. "This one. What do you think?" It was a passport picture of a very handsome young man with high cheekbones and a dark moustache. "Gemma's brother?"

"She never mentioned brothers."

"A cousin, perhaps? A boyfriend?"

"Your father, Mama?" Becca gently asked the question they'd all been thinking.

"I don't know. She never spoke of any husband. Or any family at all. Only that everyone in the castle had fallen asleep and she had been rescued by the prince."

"Obsessive-compulsive," Howie said.

"Talk to us about teeth, Weisman," Sylvia warned.

There were newspaper clippings, several more photographs of the same woman in a background filled with people as poorly dressed as she, and a small black velvet bag. Mrs. Berlin opened the bag with trembling hands, drawing out a man's ring with a large, dark stone. She passed it to Becca.

"Maybe that was our grandfather's ring," said Sylvia.

"The prince?" Howie asked. "Or Mr. Prinz?"

"I don't think she . . . well, I'm not sure she . . . I wonder if she even *knew* who my father was," Mrs. Berlin said. "It was the war. Things were crazy. She just managed to get out in time."

"In time? But Mama," Becca said, "the date on that entry form is August 14, 1944. She didn't get here until the *middle* of the war."

"That can't be right," Mrs. Berlin said, looking puzzled.

"Maybe Gemma isn't Gitl," Mike said. "After all, you never heard her called that."

"Then why keep the form?" Dr. Berlin asked.

Becca held the ring up to the light and gasped. "Mama, there's something written in the inside."

Dr. Berlin took the ring from her and went into his study, emerging with a magnifying glass in hand. "There are three letters and a date—JMP 1928."

"Not Gitl and not Mandlestein," said Mike, looking a bit satisfied.

"It's a man's ring, idiot," Sylvia said, but she said it with obvious fondness. "P for Prinz."

"What does it all mean?" Shana asked.

"Only Gemma knew," said Dr. Berlin.

"And it's too late to ask her," Mike added.

"Unless you believe in ghosts," Becca said. "And Benjamin assures me that we Jews don't."

"Obsessive-compulsive."

"Shut up, Howie," the three sisters said together.

Dr. Berlin set the ring down next to the photo of the woman and the child. "It's a riddle wrapped in a mystery inside an enigma."

"Russia," said Sylvia.

"Churchill," added Shana.

"That's my girls!" Dr. Berlin smiled.

"I'm going to solve it." Becca put her hand over the ring, covering the picture as well. "The riddle and the mystery and the enigma. I'm going to find the castle and the prince and reclaim our heritage. These pictures and this ring and all this other stuff will help me. I promised Gemma."

"Obsessive-compulsive," Howie tried again.

This time they all ignored him.

CHAPTER

5

Becca had a friend overnight for the first time and Gemma promised them a story at bedtime.

"She'll tell Sleeping Beauty if we ask," Becca said. "She tells it best."

The part about the curse frightened them both.

"When you are seventeen," Gemma said the wicked fairy said, "my curse will come true. You will lie down and a great mist will cover the castle and everyone will die. You, too, princess." And then Gemma gave a witch's laugh, high and horrible.

"Quick, Gemma, say the rest of it," Becca begged, half hidden under the covers, her friend Shirley spooned around her.

"What about the spinning wheel? What about the needle?" Shirley whispered, her breath stirring Becca's hair and blowing hotly against her neck.

Becca elbowed her into silence.

"But one of the good fairies," Gemma said, "had saved a wish. 'Not everyone will die. A few will just sleep. You, princess, will be one.' "

Shirley sat up in bed, furious. "That's not how it goes. You've got it wrong."

Gemma smiled.

"That's how it goes in this house," Becca said. "And if you don't like it, you're not my best friend any more."

"I want to go home," Shirley said. "I don't feel good. My tummy hurts and my throat wants to swallow up."

They took her home. She and Becca remained friends in school but she never stayed overnight again. Becca never invited her.

CHAPTER

6

The house was silent when Becca got up, except for the ticking of the grandfather clock in the hall. She had not been able to sleep. The room had seemed too hot and she'd thrown off the covers with a sweeping, almost imperial gesture. Not five minutes later, the room was freezing and she had to scrabble around recovering both blanket and quilt. After two hours of successively sweating and shivering, she gave up and got up, checking the clock-radio on her bedside table. As she watched, the numbers ticked over from 1:59 to 2:00. Sighing, she put her feet over the side of the bed, feeling around for her slippers. Then she went downstairs, belting her flannel robe as she went.

She got out a handful of chocolate chip cookies from the blue-and-white cookie jar and padded into the living room. Clicking through the thirty-six cable stations, she found three soft-core movies, one of which she'd already seen, some stale news, and the weather channel promising rain in Texas and a heat wave in Phoenix. When she found herself staring at a test pattern for more than a few seconds, she clicked off the television with rather more vehemence than warranted, and went back into the kitchen.

The cookie jar was empty except for three stale Fig Newtons. She hated Fig Newtons, even when they weren't stale, but she ate them anyway.

Wandering into the dining room, she turned on the light. The patchwork of papers still littered the table. She walked around the table slowly, trying to pretend the collection of old photos and mysterious forms and newspaper clippings were not worth a night's sleep.

"Gemma was just not *there* in the end," she whispered. "This means nothing." It didn't surprise her that the inflections were Sylvia's and not her own.

She pulled out a chair and sat at the head of the table by the wooden box. After a minute, she put her hand on the boxtop and pressed down, hard enough so that the carving of briar and rose imprinted on her palm. When she looked at her hand she could see the outline clearly.

"It's no good," she whispered, meaning it was no good trying to convince herself the pieces of paper were unimportant. The fact that Gemma had them tucked away in a box all these years, carrying the box with her to the nursing home, *had* to mean something. Gemma. Genevieve. Dawna. Gitl. Briar Rose. Whoever.

All at once, as if the words were being spoken aloud, she heard her grandmother telling the story of Sleeping Beauty. The room was suddenly filled with it:

> *Once upon a time, which is all times and no times*
> *but not the very best of times, there was a castle. . . .*
> *and the queen went to bed and gave birth to a baby*
> *girl with a crown of red hair.*

Becca touched her own springy red hair and smiled. She and Gemma, the family roses, Daddy called them. Like most redheads, Becca hadn't had a full head of hair until she was nearly two. But in fairy tales *anything* was possible. She looked around guiltily, in case anyone had seen her gesture. But no one else was up.

*So the king said it was time for a party with cake
and ice cream and golden plates. And not to mention
invitations sent to all the good fairies in the kingdom. But not the bad fairy. Not the one in black with
big black boots and silver . . .*

"Eagles," Becca said aloud. She wondered, and not for the
first time, if her own ability to tell a story, to invent details, came from Gemma. *Inventing details* was not a gift
a journalist should cultivate.

*"I curse you and your father the king and your
mother the queen and all your uncles and cousins
and aunts. . . . And all the people who bear your
name. . . .*

Becca shuddered. It was only a story after all; she had
heard it a hundred hundred times. But suddenly it occurred
to her that, in fact, Gemma had had no one else who bore
her name. No mother, no father, no . . . husband. Only a
daughter who had three daughters. Maybe that was why
she had been so obsessed with the story of Briar Rose.
Just a fairy tale, she whispered to herself, a kind of comfort. But in this house of death it was no comfort at all.

The good fairy had promised not death, but sleep. And
after all, what was so bad about sleeping? She and Shana
and Sylvia had talked about it over and over.

And then, all at once, Becca's childhood question was
answered. "It's not the sleeper who minds. It's the ones
left behind, awake."

Gemma's story never ended happily ever after except
for the princess Briar Rose and her own little girl. There
had always been something decidedly odd about the whole
telling. Only now was Becca able to admit it. In Gemma's
story everyone—other than the prince who wakes the princess with a kiss and Briar Rose and afterwards their
child—*everyone* else sleeps on. But what about . . . and

Gemma's voice came back, the dark words tumbling across the dining room:

> *Everyone slept: lords and ladies, teachers and tummlers, dogs and doves, rabbits and rabbitzen and all kinds of citizens ...*

Becca took a deep breath and the sounds of Gemma's words seemed to fade. In the storybooks she'd read in school, everyone got to wake up at the prince's kiss. But in Gemma's version, the implication was that they all still slept under the wicked fairy's sentence of death. Death by sleep. No wonder Shirley what's-her-name who had lived down the block never wanted to come back and sleep over at the house again. Death by sleep.

"Gemma, what *can* you have been thinking of!" Becca said fiercely. Then she yawned and picked up the photograph of the woman and child. "And did *you* live happily ever after?" she asked it. The woman stared straight out at the camera, her black eyes gazing past Becca. No matter how Becca moved the photo, the woman's eyes stared over her shoulder. The child, a finger in her mouth like a stopper, lay with closed eyes, head on her mother's breast.

By the time the others were straggling down to breakfast, Becca had organized the contents of the box, falling asleep at the table, her head resting between two of four piles. One pile was photographs, the second clippings, the third documents, and the fourth what she called "others": That included the ring, an envelope with two curls of hair, one gold and one red, a brass button, possibly from a uniform, and the torn half of an Italian train ticket.

The clippings she had arranged in chronological order, the first from August 30, 1944, the last from June 3, 1956.

The photographs were impossible to date. Only one had any kind of identification at all, though the same young woman appeared in each. She was clearly pregnant in all the photographs except the one in which she was holding the child. In all but that picture she was wearing the same dress, a shapeless dark dress with white piping at the collar and sleeves. They showed her standing a little apart from other people in front of a row of barracks, a bit of a lake or ocean appearing in the background, behind the buildings. In each shot she held her right hand protectively over her belly and looked warily to the side of the photographer.

It was the documents that Becca puzzled over the longest, seven in all. One was the entry form into America with the same date as the oldest newspaper clipping. Another was a white paper, 8½ by 14, with Gitl Mandlestein's signature in careful penmanship at the bottom. It looked like a kind of visa. There was a birth certificate for Eve Stein, a certificate of citizenship with a photo of a solemn and still young Dawna Stein dated July 6, 1946, a rental agreement for an apartment on Twelfth Street and Avenue A in New York City, and an Immunization Register. Finally, bound in pale blue, there was a mortgage document for the house on School Street where Becca and her sisters had grown up. Gemma had bought it in 1953 for $8,500. Thirty-eight years ago.

"Signposts," Becca had whispered, turning each one over. But why had Gemma kept them secret? And what had any of them to do with the story of Briar Rose?

"Gemma, I'm trying," she had whispered to the silent room before falling asleep at the table, head on her hands.

It was her mother who found her and woke her gently. "Becca—go on to bed. You'll just make yourself sick this way. And I can't deal with you being sick right now."

She blinked owlishly up at her mother, then sighed. "Only promise you won't move anything? I have it all arranged. Promise you'll keep them out of the piles." By *them* she meant her sisters.

"But what about breakfast?"

"Eat in the kitchen, like always. Never mind what they say." Sylvia had complained once about how unsophisticated it was to eat at the kitchen table, but that was after she had married Mike and they had a live-in nanny for Benjamin. Sylvia had taken French cooking lessons; she ate with candles. "Promise?"

"I promise, dear."

Only then did Becca grudgingly go up to bed, but her sleep was fitful, disturbed by the screams of the three children as they raced up and down the stairs and through the halls.

CHAPTER

7

"Why do you tell Sleeping Beauty all the time, Gemma?" Becca asked on the day she graduated from kindergarten. They were seated at a Friendly's in Northampton and Becca's stomach was tight with the strawberry fribble. Some of it had dribbled down her dress front. She was glad Shana and Sylvia were still in school, otherwise they would have teased her. "Fribble dribble!" they would have chanted all the way home.

"Don't you like Sleeping Beauty?" Gemma asked.

"I like it. But why do you say it all the time?" Becca had persisted.

"Because I like it, too," Gemma said.

She had told it in the car on the way home. And when she got to the part where the king said: "Sing and dance, my people. Sing and dance. Keep all thoughts of the mist away. I forbid you to think about it," Becca said it with her.

"And do you know the next part?" Gemma asked.

"I do, I do!" Becca said.

"Well, as it is your graduation from kindergarten, and next year you will be in hard school ..."—hard school was what Shana and Sylvia called it because they had *homework*—*"you will probably not want to hear my little story ever again."*

Becca had leaned over, putting her hand on her grandmother's arm. *"I will want to hear it* always, *Gemma. Because it is* your *story."*

"From your lips to God's ears," Gemma said.

"That's not from this *part of the story, silly Gemma,"* Becca said. And as her grandmother smiled, Becca spoke the next part of the tale.

"When princess Briar Rose was seventeen—that's tenlevens more than me, Gemma."

"That's twelve more than you."

"When princess Briar Rose was seventeen, one day and without further warning . . . What's a warning?"

"Telling you to watch out."

"Oh! Without further warning, a mist covered the entire kingdom. What's a mist?"

"A fog. An exhaust."

"A mist. A great mist. It covered the entire kingdom. And everyone in it—the good people and the not-so-good, the young people and the not-so-young, and even Briar Rose's mother and father fell asleep. Everyone slept: lords and ladies, teacher and tummlers, dogs and doves, rabbits and rabbitzen and all kinds of citizens. So fast asleep they were, they were not able to wake up for a hundred years. Are you a hundred years, Gemma?"

"Not yet."

"I'm six."

"Not yet."

"Is a hundred a lot?"

"A hundred years is forever."

CHAPTER

8

By the time Becca got up it was noon. Sun streamed in through the slats of the blinds, making familiar and comfortable patterns on the floor. She knew she had dreamed lots of short dreams all through the night, a veritable anthology of them, but she couldn't recall any. Stretching, she got up and did a quick ten floor touches and ten deep-knee bends, then went to the bathroom to brush her teeth.

The bathroom door was shut and she could hear Howie humming to himself inside. A light tap on the door brought no response, so she shrugged and went downstairs. She supposed coffee could disguise the bad taste in her mouth as well as toothpaste.

The kitchen sink was piled high with breakfast dishes, and the coffeepot was empty, which meant her mother was back in bed. She filled the pot, got out a new filter, threw the old one onto the garbage, and counted out five tablespoons of Columbian Supreme. Then she waited while the magic of modern invention turned tap water into a hot dark-brown caffeine-powered drink. It was better than any Biblical miracle and risked no beliefs. While she waited, she rinsed the dishes and put them in the dishwasher.

A small body careened in through the door. "Aunt Becca, he's chaaaaasing me."

"Not now, Sarah," Becca said, "your grandmother's in bed." But she knelt anyway to enclose her niece in the safety of her arms.

Benjamin raced in, braking to a stop when he saw Becca. Then he pouted. "No fair. No grownups."

"I haven't had my coffee yet," Becca warned.

Benjamin turned and raced out and Sarah, peeling herself out of Becca's arms, followed screaming, "I'm gonna get *you*!"

"Coffee!" Howie walked into the room and poured himself a large mug of it, sipped it down, then topped it off again.

Becca stood and rescued the rest of the coffee for herself, then quickly started another potful. "Howie," she began slowly, "do you . . ."

"Not till I drink my coffee, Becca. Are you making breakfast?" His voice was childlike, wheedling.

Pointedly ignoring him, she walked into the dining room. Her mother had kept her promise; the four piles were as Becca had left them, inviolate. She sat down, putting the coffee mug on a coaster, and stared at the pieces of paper. Finally she picked up the photo of Gemma and the child as if by touching it she might get some kind of clue. The more she stared at the woman in the picture, the less the woman looked like Gemma, just some ill-dressed stranger from a half-century past.

When she finally took a sip of the coffee, it was lukewarm and she made a face. Then she pushed the four piles together, sweeping them back into the carved box. Hefting the box she wondered how—as frail as Gemma had been—she had managed to cart the box to the nursing home; stranger still that Mama had never seen it before. But she remembered suddenly that a visiting nurse had helped Gemma pack. And Gemma had always been secretive about things. Certainly about the past.

"A riddle wrapped in a mystery inside an enigma." It

was her father coming in to sit beside her, clutching a coffee mug.

"Churchill," she said automatically. Then she added, "And Gemma."

He reached over and patted her hand.

Still holding the box, she stood and kissed him on the top of the head. "I'm going over to the *Advocate*."

"Honey, it's just the day after the funeral. Nobody expects you at work. And your mother wants the family to sit shiva for the full seven days."

"I'm not going to work to *work*, Daddy," she said. "I'm going to think."

"About that box." He inclined his head towards it.

She nodded. "About the box. About its contents. And about our riddle. About . . ."

"About Briar Rose." He nodded back. "Besides, it's hard to think in the house with Shana and Sylvia here. If I hadn't already canceled all my operations . . ." He chuckled. When their eyes met it was as if they shared a family secret. "Go on. I'll cover for you."

"Thanks, Daddy. You're a peach. The peachiest."

"I, on the other hand, have no favorites," he reminded her, mock serious.

"I know, Daddy, I know." She smiled as she left.

Even though the box was heavy and awkward, Becca decided to walk. The day was unaccountably mild and the newspaper was housed in a building that was only two country blocks away.

As she made the turn on School Street, she saw Dr. Grenzke weeding the herbacious borders by his house. He waved but the box was too heavy to shift so she just shouted a greeting back. By the time she passed Monty's grocery with its cheery neon beer sign and the hand-lettered poster advertising a tag sale, the corner of the box was beginning to dig into her side. She was afraid to shift it for fear of dropping it, so she set it on the sidewalk, then picked it up again, long-ways around.

By the Polish Club, she had to put the box down once more. When she knelt this time, a chorus of whistles floated down from the porch. She looked up, ready to say something sharp, and laughed. It was Mr. Stowkowski and his son Jamie. Jamie had been a year ahead of her in high school and they'd gone to the junior prom together. He and his father were in construction, Jamie the plural part of Stowkowski and Sons. Soon to be *grandsons*, she reminded herself. Jamie's girlfriend was pregnant.

"Shouldn't you two be at work?" she called out, standing once again with the box.

"Break!" they called out together. Eerily their voices were exactly alike.

She laughed and walked on.

The *Advocate* was housed in an old remodeled mill overlooking the Mill River's waterfall. New Englanders, her father often remarked, were very conservative when it came to place names. There were at least seven Mill Rivers in Massachusetts and Connecticut that he knew of. The building was always bustling with gossip and a revolutionary ardor indistinguishable from religious fervor in its intensity. As Jonathan Edwards had been the minister in nearby Northampton two centuries earlier, such ardor seemed appropriate. But since the advent of computers in the newsroom, things had become quite a bit quieter. Now the constant *basso* of the waterfall was broken only by the ringing of the phones and an occasional burst of laughter. An alternative newspaper, the *Advocate* came out once a week so the laughter was of the frantic variety. As Shana had exclaimed when Becca first got the job there, "It's free to everyone except its advertisers. Hope you actually get paid." And Sylvia had added when she heard, "Even the Revolution has to pay its bills!"

Becca's first professional bylines—she didn't count the ones for the Smith College *Sophian*—had appeared in the *Advocate*: a full-page article on the local shelter for battered women, Jessie's House, and a page and a half on Merlin Brooks, who wrote lesbian science fiction at her

farm in Montague. Merlin had been Becca's writing
teacher for one semester at Smith before politics and a
nervous Board of Trustees had conspired to kick her out.
The signs Becca had posted all over campus (FREE MER-
LIN BROOKS and KEEP THE MAGIC AT SMITH) in
time for reunion weekend and the two pieces she wrote for
the *Sophian*—sharp angry pieces—had made Becca a campus celebrity. And a friend of Merlin's for life. ("Even if
you *are* straight," Merlin had told her in that unfortunate
squeaky little-girl voice. "Even if you don't have a sense
of the ironic.")

The box was unbearably heavy by the time she reached
the *Advocate*. Swollen by spring rains, the waterfall was
cascading loudly over its rocks and Becca turned for a moment to look at it. Even the box's weight could not stop
her from her regular obeisance to the falls. But when she
finally pushed through the door into the reception area and
lowered the box on the receptionist's desk, she greeted
Merelle with a long sigh:

"There," she said.

Merelle looked up and covered the mouthpiece of the
phone. "Hi, Bec. Sorry to hear about your grandmother.
But I thought you were taking the week off."

"Thanks. I am."

"Then why are you here? No," she said hastily into the
phone, "not you, sir. I'm sorry." She covered the mouthpiece more carefully and looked at Becca expectantly.

"To get away from home," Becca said.

Merelle nodded in understanding. She came from a family of nine. "Now, sir, what can I do for . . ."

Lifting the box once more, this time to her shoulder,
Becca went up the stairs to her own desk. She nodded at
the other reporters as she went, effectively cutting off any
expressions of condolence. Most of them had sent cards
anyway. This time when she put the box down, it was as
if a great burden had really been lifted from her shoulders.
She smiled wryly to herself and whispered, "Walking metaphor. Merlin would be so pleased."

"Talking to me?"

She turned around. In the doorway of his office was Stan, her editor, leaning casually against the jamb.

"No." She shook her head. "Just calling myself all kinds of fool." She touched her hand to her hair. Being around Stan always made her do things like that: fix her hair, smooth down her skirt, tug the sweater over her jeans. He made her feel part schoolgirl, part coquette. Not that he actually said or did anything. It was just his *presence*. Thirty-five years old and thinned down to bone; wire-rimmed glasses that only magnified the blue of his eyes; straight brown hair cut short but never in any recognizable style, as if he trimmed it himself in front of a half-mirror; a nose that was short and straight and unremarkable. And a low voice with an edge to it that always threatened laughter behind its intensity. She didn't understand why he made her feel so left-footed. It wasn't as if he were actually devastatingly attractive.

"What arc you doing here anyway? You said the other day you wanted to take the week off."

"I was. I am."

"Which is it?"

"You sound like a Jewish mother."

He laughed. They both knew he was pure Yankee, an Episcopalian who hadn't seen the inside of a church since high school. It was his one boast. "Well . . . ?"

Her hand strayed to her hair again and she willed it to return and touch the box instead. She opened the lid. "My grandmother had this with her at the nursing home. It's filled with . . . with documents and stuff. I thought it might tell me who she really was."

"What do you mean—who she really was? She was a nice lady, a Jewish grandmother, who walked around the block in rain, sleet, or snow every single day of the year. A Hatfield landmark. *Who she was*. Do you think she was a spy? A Russian mole? A runner of guns for the Irgun? A mafioso moll? Harlan Ellison's secret muse? Or perhaps

you think she had a sleazy past on New York's Forty-
second Street."

Becca knew he was trying to make her laugh but all she
could do was shrug. "Damned if I know."

"Well, what do your parents say?"

"Damned if they know either."

"Really?" His head cocked to one side.

"Really."

He left the doorway and came over and sat on her desk,
waiting. He was good at waiting.

Becca touched the box again as if touching a talisman.
"No one really knows where she came from. She never
said. She—this is going to sound dumb. . . ."

"Say it. I won't care. If it's dumb and the facts bear
it out, then you're a genius. If it's dumb and the facts
don't bear it out, saying it won't make it any dumber. Or
you."

Becca looked up at the ceiling and drew a deep breath.
"Sometimes I wonder if *she* really knew where she came
from."

"Everyone knows where they came from, Becca. Or do
you mean she was adopted? I was adopted. But I know
where I came from. I know my adoptive parents and my
birth mother, too. It was the first story I ever chased down.
I was fourteen."

"I didn't know that," she whispered.

He shrugged as if giving her back whatever pity or awe
she might be feeling. "So what do you mean? Really?"

Becca opened the box and stared down at its contents.
"I'm not sure. Except she always spoke of her past as if
it were a fairy tale."

He put his hand on the lid of the open box and looked
down into the pile of things. "A fairy tale?"

"Briar Rose. You know—Sleeping Beauty. She always
insisted that she was the princess in the castle and that a
mist came over the entire castle and everyone fell asleep.
She was the only one kissed awake by the prince."

"*Always?*" He leaned forward and the space between

them suddenly seemed charged. It wasn't personal; she'd
learned that long ago. He always leaned forward when he
was interested in a story, making the moment electric. It
made him a great editor. "She *always* spoke of it that
way?"

Becca shifted away from him slightly and tried to answer with a coolness she didn't feel. "If you mean before
she got sick—yes. *Always*. At least as long as I can remember."

He leaned back, considering. At last he spoke. "What
do the facts say, Becca?" He began fingering the top
paper, the visa. "Any castles in the family? Any palaces?
Or at least a mansion?" He picked the visa up and scanned
it.

"She didn't have any money to speak of, Stan," Becca
answered. "We always thought she came to America before the war, but evidently she came in 1944. She worked
real hard, scrimping and saving all her life. She was still
working hard up until the time she got so . . . sick. Until
she started forgetting things and *had* to stop."

"Anastasia didn't have any money," Stan said quietly.
"Any deposed royalty is without its castles and palaces
and . . ."

"She was *Jewish*, for God's sake, Stan!"

He smiled. "*And* she had a visa that let her into the
country in the middle of the war. Maybe she was a
Rothschild. It was difficult getting in here without the
right connections—family or friends to sponsor you.
Maybe she *worked* for the Rothschild's at a castle or palace or mansion. And what about that prince?"

She shook her head. "We don't even know if she was
married." Unaccountably her eyes filled with tears.

Stan reached over with gentle fingers, raised her chin,
and stared at her. "My birth mother wasn't married, Becca.
What does that make me?" He shook his head. "So you've
found no castles, no princes. At least none yet. Except
those in the fairy tale. I'm sorry about your grandmother,

Becca. The times I met her, I liked her. But you have only begun to investigate this story."

He stood and went back to his office, whistling. She recognized the tune. It was Sondheim's "Into the Woods." She'd seen the play at UMass last semester. Biting her lower lip lightly, she realized she could still feel the pressure of his fingers on her chin.

It took her fifteen minutes to re-sort the piles, but when she was done, she felt the same kind of focusing that attended the start of any new story. Looking again at the entry form and at the newspaper clipping from the same date, she sighed. The clipping was from the *Palladium Times*, the dateline Oswego. The clipping was no more than some kind of local news report about a town council. There was an ad on the back. She wasn't even sure where Oswego was, except somewhere in New York State. She went over to the bookcase where the state maps were kept.

Oswego was on Lake Ontario, halfway between Rochester and Syracuse. *Editor and Publisher* gave her the listing for the *Palladium Times*.

As she dialed the number, she whispered "Lake Ontario" aloud, thinking about the water behind the buildings in the photograph. "What *am* I doing?" she added, underlining the number of the newspaper with sharp heavy strokes in time to the ringing phone.

The second person she talked to was a reporter. She introduced herself.

"So, how can I help you, reporter to reporter?" the man asked.

"Why do you suppose," Becca mused aloud, "that my grandmother would have kept a clipping from a 1944 *Palladium-Times*?"

"Beats me," the man said. "Grandmothers can be real strange. Take mine, for example. She collected wasp nests. Among other things."

"A clipping from the same date as her entry visa," Becca added.

"Entry visa?"

"Yes—is that important?" Becca asked.

"She was some kind of war refugee, you mean?" The man hesitated.

"Some kind," Becca said, a cold shiver going down her back, the kind of shiver she got whenever she was closing in on an important detail of a story. "I just don't know what kind."

"Well, maybe it's not related at all," he said, "but Oswego was the only war refugee shelter in America. Fort Oswego. Roosevelt made it a camp and in August 1944 some one thousand people were brought over and interned here. From Naples, Italy. Mostly Jews and about one hundred Christians. We ran a number of articles about it recently. It's quite a story actually. They're turning the Fort into a museum and—"

Becca found herself gripping the phone so hard, her fingers hurt. "Can you send me copies of the articles?"

"Sure thing, honey. Just give me your name and address."

She let the *honey* go by and told him what he needed to know.

"By the way," he continued, "besides the articles I have a couple of addresses you might want. Wait a minute . . ." She could hear him rooting around his desk, muttering some colorful curses. "The National Archives . . . where is that frig-footed . . . there it is. It's in Washington, D.C., and will have material on the shelter, documents and all. Under the War Refugee Board, I think it was. Or the War Relocation Authority."

Becca scribbled the names on her pad.

"What isn't in the articles, they might have."

"Thanks."

"My pleasure. My grandmother died just last month. You wouldn't *believe* the stuff we found in her closet. Some of it . . . well . . . pretty surprising."

"I'm sure," Becca said warmly.

"In fact, *incredibly* surprising," he said.

"Can you send those articles soon?" Becca asked.

"They're already in the mail," he said. "Anything else, just give me a call. That's Arnie, with an i-e. Professional courtesy and all."

CHAPTER

9

"*All around the castle,*" *Gemma said, making tucking-in motions though they were all in sleeping bags in the big tent, "a briary hedge began to grow, with thorns as sharp as barbs.*"

"*What's barbs, Gemma?*" *Syl asked. "You never tell us what barbs are.*"

"*Better you shouldn't know.*"

"*But we want to know, Gemma,*" *Shana said. "We want to know it all.*"

Little Becca, second finger in her mouth, was already half asleep. From the smaller tent came the sound of Dr. Berlin and his wife talking cozily.

Ignoring the question, Gemma continued the tale. "Higher and higher the thorny bush grew until it covered the windows and it covered the doors. It covered the high castle towers and no one could see in and—"

"*And no one could see out,*" *Sylvia said. "But you didn't say about the barbs.*"

"*I want to hear the story,*" *Shana said, nudging her sister.*

"*And no one could see out,*" *Gemma said, oblivious to*

the two, watching the sleeping Becca as she spoke. "And no one cared to know about the sleeping folk inside."

"I want to know about the barbs," said Sylvia.

"Shut up," Shana said.

"Gemma, she said shut up."

"Did not."

"Did."

"And no one cared to know about the sleeping folk inside," Gemma said pointedly. "So no one told about them and neither will I."

"Now you've done it," Sylvia said.

"You did, too," said Shana. "Please, Gemma. Pretty please. With strawberries on it. And roses."

But Gemma could not be persuaded to finish the story that night.

CHAPTER

10

It was ten days before Arnie—with an i-e—sent the clippings. The prose was flat and Becca found she had to force herself to go through them, underlining possible salient points with a yellow marker. The National Archives had—surprisingly—sent a packet that arrived the same day. Becca worked on them at the dining room table that evening.

The house was quiet, Sylvia and Shana and their families having at last gone home, more reluctantly than Becca could have possibly guessed. Shana had made her swear to call if she felt even the slightest bit blue and Sylvia had slipped a check for two hundred dollars into her pocket, whispering, "Buy something for yourself, Becca. *Just* for you."

As she sat shuffling through the papers, her father went past on his way into the kitchen. "You are going to wear that stuff out," he commented wryly. "All those years your grandmother hoarded those documents and clippings and within two weeks of her death they are going to crumble from overuse."

"Leave her alone, Jerold," her mother said, following him into the kitchen. "A promise is a promise."

They went into the kitchen and out the other door, arguing companionably about popcorn, while Becca settled back to the table full of papers. Arnie Salembier's articles about the Fort Oswego shelter told her little that seemed important to her grandmother's past except that it gave her a possible starting place. The National Archives, on the other hand, had sent a whole packet of forms relating to the Oswego shelter, including biographical data sheets. They'd had no information about Dawna Stein or even Dawna Mandlestein or Genevieve Mandlestein. But they had hit pay dirt with Gitl.

BIOGRAPHICAL DATA CONCERNING ALLIED, NATIONAL, OR NEUTRAL headed the first sheet. Gitl Mandlestein had been married, had lived last in Poland, was white, was Jewish, was able to work—all filled in with a steady hand. But the date of that marriage had been left blank, the village and district in Poland had not been noted, and employment and education questions had not been answered. Where it asked: HAS REGISTRANT A HOME TO WHICH HE DESIRES TO RETURN? the answer had been left blank as well. The sheet was dated 1944.

"Gitl," Becca whispered. "Gitl Mandlestein. Your life seems to be mostly blank. How can I possibly fill it in nearly fifty years later? How do I even know you are my grandmother? My Gemma?"

There was a loud braying laugh from the TV room. Her father always enjoyed himself to the fullest. If the laugh was an answer, it was not the one she wanted to hear.

WHAT IS YOUR TRUE AND CORRECT NAME? Gitl Rose Mandlestein.

"Rose?" Becca said. "Really? So—elementary, my dear Watsonstein!"

IF YOU ARE A MARRIED WOMAN WHAT WAS YOUR MAIDEN NAME? Gitl Rose Mandlestein.

"Didn't you understand the question, Gitl? Was the English too hard?" Becca asked.

BY WHAT NAMES HAVE YOU ALSO BEEN

KNOWN: (INCLUDE PROFESSIONAL NAMES OR
ANY OTHER NAMES BY WHICH YOU HAVE BEEN
KNOWN.) Księżniczka.

"And Eve. Dawna. Gemma."

WHAT WAS YOUR LAST PERMANENT ADDRESS?
The answer was crossed out with a single dark stroke.

MALE. FEMALE. (x) HEIGHT: 5 foot. WEIGHT: 139
pounds. HAIR: red. EYES blue.

"It *has* to be Gemma. Height, hair color, eyes. Weight
. . . that's much too heavy," Becca thought, sighing. The
rest of the questions were mostly left unanswered: father's
name, mother's name, age. Didn't she know them? Or had
she been hiding something? And why should she hide, now
that her war was over, now that she was safe in America,
safe in Fort Oswego, safe in a shelter? It made no sense.

Under the heading IF YOU HAVE ANY LIVING
CHILDREN, in a peculiarly Germanic italic hand, someone had written, "With child, due any day."

"Maybe . . ." Becca said, standing, "maybe that explains
the weight." She stretched and headed toward the TV
room. It was a commercial break and her father had silenced the set with the remote clicker. He was offering the
bucket of popcorn to his wife when Becca came in.

"Mom—exactly when were you born?"

"Exactly August thirtieth dear. I thought you knew that.
You give me a present every year."

"I mean—what year?"

"Why, 1944. Is it important?"

The TV clicked on again to the aggressive theme music
of *L.A. Law.*

" 'Due any day,' " Becca explained.

"What dear?" her mother asked over the sound of Michael Tucker and his wife quarreling.

"Maybe," Becca said, raising her voice a little, "from
August 14 to August 30 was simply 'any day.' "

"So you think Gitl Mandlestein was your grandmother and
she came from somewhere in Poland," Stan said the next

morning, running a bony hand through his hair. He pursed his lips and thought a minute. "And that other name by which she was known—Księżniczka—any ideas?"

"No. I've never heard it before."

"Is it Yiddish?" he asked.

"Probably Polish." She shrugged. "At a guess."

"Don't guess. Find out. It's your only lead." He stared thoughtfully at her.

Becca had to look away.

Stan went into his office and closed the door and Becca leaned back in her chair. The comforting, familiar sounds surrounded her, helped her think. In between writing a story on a local factory strike and organizing the list of the Best of the Valley poll, she'd worked on her grandmother's papers. In her mind she could hear Howie's nasal voice warning, "Obsessive-compulsive!" and her father cautioning her against wearing out the tattered forms. But Stan had been the one to urge her to continue.

When he saw her hunched over the papers that morning, he'd sat on her desk and leaned forward. "Stories," he'd said, his voice low and almost husky, "we are made up of stories. And even the ones that seem the most like lies can be our deepest hidden truths. I don't think you're going to be happy until you find out who your grandmother was, Becca. Just as I couldn't be happy until I found my birth mother."

She picked up the phone and called the Town Hall.

When the clerk answered, Becca greeted her warmly.

"Sorry about your grandmother," the clerk said.

"Thanks. It's about her, actually," Becca answered.

"What about?"

"She was called Księżniczka at one time. I think that's Polish and I know you spoke Polish at home." She spelled it.

The clerk chuckled. "What an awful hash you've made of the pronunciation."

"To many c's and z's," Becca said by way of excuse. "Is it a common name?"

"Not a name, really. It's pronounced Kshen-zhních-kah. With a nasal 'n' like in French. Means princess."

Becca was stunned. "It means *princess*?" she said at last.

"Like in king and queen and . . ." the clerk said. "A *young* princess, actually. There's a different word for an old princess. Księżniczka."

"Gesundheit!" Becca answered. They both laughed. But as Becca put down the phone, her heart was pounding. Gemma's middle name had been Rose and her other—nickname? alias? code name?—had been *princess*.

"So, Watsonstein," she said to herself, "what's so elementary now?"

She stared at her grandmother's papers for another hour, but could get nothing more from them and, at last, pushed them reluctantly to one side to work on the strike story instead. There she had more facts than she needed; everyone involved had wanted to talk about the issues. It was the focus she hadn't got yet.

By noon, her brain felt scrubbed, as if she had already worked an entire day.

Taking her yogurt out to the side of the waterfall, she sat down on the still-cold ground. The pounding of the water over the rocks blocked out everything except the quarreling of two housefinches over yesterday's crumbs.

"I'd give you this," she said to the birds, holding out the half-finished yogurt, "but I don't think it's your style."

"Why not? I like yogurt." Stan squatted down by her side, the noise of his arrival having been disguised by the water's insistent boom. He took the container and spoon from her unresisting hand and spooned some of the strawberry yogurt into his mouth.

Startled, Becca found herself blushing unaccountably.

"Not much left," he said, looking ruefully into the cup. "I guess I'll have to go to Monty's and buy my own." He grinned slowly and handed the container back. "How's that story?"

"Lots of facts, no focus," she said.

"Thought you didn't have any real leads."

For a moment, she was confused, then realized he was talking about her grandmother. "Oh—*that* story. I found out that Księżniczka . . ." she stumbled over the pronunciation, "means princess."

"Gesundheit!" he said.

She giggled.

"Princess. Hmmmmm. I think I'm liking this story more and more. But I don't think we can talk about it at work. Can I come over this evening and look at the papers with you?"

"No. Yes. I mean . . ." The flush on her face deepened; she could tell just from the generated heat on her cheeks.

"Good," he said, not seeming to notice. "I'll be there after dinner. About seven?"

"Sure," she began, but he was already standing and striding across the lawn toward the street. She watched until he was out of sight. When she looked down at the yogurt container, she saw it was empty. That didn't stop her from running her finger around the inside and popping the finger into her mouth, licking it sensuously and thinking about nothing at all.

CHAPTER

11

"It took a hundred years," said Gemma.

"Why, Gemma? Why a hundred years?" Becca asked. They were peeling apples in preparation for making applesauce. Gemma made the best applesauce, better even than store-bought, Becca thought. Sylvia and Shana hated it though.

"It's lumpy," Shana said. "It's bumpy."

"It's got the pips," Sylvia added, giggled, then refused to eat her share.

"A hundred years, a thousand years," Gemma said. "It doesn't matter. Dead is dead."

"But they weren't dead," Sylvia reminded her. "Just sleeping."

"That's why a hundred years then," Gemma said. "It took a hundred years and then a prince of a nearby country . . ."

"Was it America?" asked Becca, America being the only country she knew about.

"Was it England?" Sylvia was in hard school. She knew these things.

"Was it France?" Shana was, too.

"*I see England, I see France . . .*" Sylvia said. "*I see Shana's underpants.*"

"*Do not.*"

"*Do, too.*"

"*Do not. Gemma, she does not.*"

"*I see them, too,*" Becca said, *though she couldn't see them and immediately felt bad about telling a fib.*

"*The prince came from a nearby country . . .*" Gemma *tried again, but even she could see that no one was listening, underpants being* much *more interesting than princes in this day and age.*

CHAPTER

12

Stan arrived exactly at seven, as if he had been waiting outside until the town clock tolled the last stroke of the hour. Becca opened the door just as promptly, not being able to bear the wait any longer.

"Dr. Berlin, Mrs. Berlin," he greeted her parents formally, almost—Becca thought—as if he were picking her up for a date.

"I have things spread out on the dining room table," she said.

"Good. Let's get to work."

"You certainly don't believe in foreplay," Dr. Berlin commented.

Becca felt her cheeks burn but Stan laughed. "Not on stories anyway," he said. "Get in, get it over with, get out."

They walked into the dining room, Becca relieved that her father just nodded and went upstairs. If he had said another word, Becca knew she would have throttled him.

"So, give me the Cook's tour," Stan said, gesturing to the pieces of paper she had so carefully arranged around the table. "A second eye and all that."

She walked him around, telling him the few facts she

had been able to glean from the photographs and the papers. When he bent over to look at a particular piece, he pushed his glasses up onto the top of his head in order to read. They went all around the table before he offered a comment.

"Pretty sparse gleanings." The glasses were back down on his nose.

She nodded.

"And you've gotten almost as much as you can from this, as far as I can tell. Time for some footwork."

"What do you mean?"

"Tomorrow is Saturday. You and I are going to visit Fort Oswego."

"But that's . . ." She had no idea how far away it was.

"Five to six hours from here. I have a friend from college who lives there. We can stay with her. I'll drive. You navigate." He grinned. "I judge people by how well they read maps."

She stopped herself from asking how *good* a friend from college the Oswego lady was. After all, it was none of her business. Instead she nodded again. "Map reading is always my job on family trips. My mother's terrible at it. She gets east and west mixed up. And Shana and Sylvia always fought too much. I got the job by default and I'm pretty good."

"Somehow I knew that," he said. "Let's make an early start. And don't forget to bring all this along. Samantha might be able to make some connections." His sweeping gesture took in everything on the table top.

"Samantha," she whispered. Of course.

"See you tomorrow morning. Seven. No later." He turned abruptly and walked to the door, calling out, "Bye, Dr. Berlin. Bye, Mrs. Berlin."

When Becca closed the door behind him, her parents were standing in the door of the family room.

"That was a mighty short date, dear," her mother said.

"It wasn't a date. We're going to Oswego tomorrow."

"Oswego?"

"In New York State," Becca explained.

"That's a good six hours from here," her father said. "Going to stay over?"

"I don't ... yes ... no ... probably."

"I told you he didn't believe in foreplay," her father said.

"Jerold!"

"We will be staying—if we stay over—with a friend of Stan's from college," Becca explained slowly, as if talking to someone in a foreign language.

"That's nice, dear. Who?" Mrs. Berlin asked.

"Her name is Samantha."

"Of course," Dr. Berlin said.

"I *am* twenty-three years old," Becca said.

"Old enough," Mrs. Berlin said and taking her husband by the arm, led him back into the family room.

Becca ran into the kitchen and got herself a glass of cold water, drinking it right down and wondering what she could possibly wear.

In the end she wore her grey wool pants because a dress would hamper exploration but jeans might be too casual for any possible interviewing. If she had expected Stan to take as much care with his appearance, she was disappointed. He arrived at seven dressed as he always did, in corduroy pants and an open-necked shirt, and the same corduroy jacket he lived in at work. There was a picnic basket in the back seat and a blanket. She didn't exactly raise her eyebrows, but he must have seen something in her face.

"It's still a little cold to sit on the ground for a picnic here," he explained. "Even if you are used to squatting by the waterfall every day, rain or shine. But we're going north. It'll be a lot colder there."

It was—and it wasn't—like a date. They talked about the weather, about politics, about safe office subjects. The closest it got to personal was when she asked Stan about the search for his birth mother. The way he stopped and started and inserted elliptical explanations, she knew it was not a story he told often. To her horror, she found herself blurting out, "Why? Why don't you ever talk about it?"

Stan was silent for a long moment, the car speeding along the highway. It seemed the longest moment Becca had ever sat through. She was just formulating an apology, knowing this had to be done with careful thought, when he sighed.

"I guess once I was done with it, once I knew who she was—and the fact that she really didn't know who my father was—I was satisfied. The story was finished. Over. Complete. I'm like that with all the stories I work on. She wasn't a part of my life and I wasn't a part of hers. I had all the answers I was going to get. So I got on with it."

"Will this be the same thing?" she asked.

"Meaning?"

"Meaning when I find the story . . ."

"*If* you find the story. You don't always, you know."

She nodded thoughtfully. "*If* I find the story—will it be over?"

"I guess that depends," he said.

"Depends on what?"

"On whether it's a happy-ever-after ending or not, like all good fairy tales," he said. He sped up to pass a line of poky cars.

"Gemma's Briar Rose never ended happy ever after."

"How did it end?" He pulled into the right lane and glanced over at her.

She shrugged. "With a kiss. And a wedding."

He laughed. "Isn't that happy? I like kisses." He paused. "And weddings."

"The prince isn't mentioned in the last line. It's as if he disappears after the ceremony. Only the princess and her baby daughter remain. Watch out!" The car ahead had suddenly slammed on its brakes.

Stan expertly braked and simultaneously turned the wheel slightly to the right. "Asshole!" he muttered.

Becca wasn't sure if he meant the driver ahead—or himself.

It was almost seven hours when they turned into Oswego, the picnic having slowed them down about an hour. Stan's picnic had consisted of pieces of barbecued chicken, wine, bread, cheese, and celery sticks. Plus two yogurts. He had forgotten the spoons.

Becca had laughed, while digging around in her purse. "Ta-da!" she'd cried, triumphantly, holding up a battered plastic spoon that had seen better days.

"A *lot* better days!" Stan said, wiping it on his shirt.

They took turns with the spoon and somehow, after that, things were much more relaxed between them.

Once they passed the first signs to Oswego, Stan handed her a piece of paper on which there was a series of directions in his untidy scrawl. Becca read them out to him with enough time to spare for the lane changes and left turns, of which there were many.

"That's my girl," he muttered, but he said it with a grin, to let her know that she was neither a girl nor his.

They slipped into a quiet residential street in the middle of the afternoon.

"There—number nineteen," Becca said, pointing. The house was from the 1930s, nondescript but comfortable-looking, and much too large for a single person. Becca wondered about that. She had studiously avoided asking very much about Samantha, and Stan had been uncharacteristically silent about her as well, except to say she was an illustrator. Of children's books. Becca suspected bunnies and duckies, an effective silencer for someone like Stan. Again, Becca wondered how *good* a friend Samantha had been. On the college paper together, he had said in passing. Had she gone from raise-the-barricades cartoons to bunnies-in-britches?

A dark-haired child came running across the lawn of number 19, her chubby cheeks spotty with the exercise. For a moment Becca hoped it was a Samantha clone. Then

she was followed by a second child, and a third. They ran
into the house next door. Becca sighed out loud.

"It *will* be good to get out and stretch," Stan said, mis-
taking the reason for her sigh.

"Yes."

They were still retrieving their overnight bags, when the
front door of number 19 opened, and a slim blonde came
onto the porch. (She *would* be blonde, Becca thought. And
slim.)

"Stan!" the blonde called, waving.

"Well, hello stranger," Stan called back, pushing his
glasses back up the bridge of his nose. "Good directions."

"Some things I'm good at," Samantha said. Somehow
Becca knew that was not *all* she was good at.

"And you must be Becca. Come on in. Have you had
lunch? Linn won't be home until seven, and the kids will
eat early, but I saved out something for a snack."

Becca felt a great grin spread over her face. *Linn*. No
wonder Samantha and Stan hadn't gotten together. "We've
had lunch, thank you. What a lovely house." She meant
every word.

Linn was equally tall and had been blond once upon a
time. He was now mostly bald. After the requisite jokes
about Linn and Sam and parties at which no one could
keep them straight, Becca confessed that she had assumed
Linn was the other half of a lesbian partnership.

"Me—gay?" Samantha had laughed at that, heartily sec-
onded by both Stan and Linn. A little *too* heartily, Becca
thought. But the others didn't seem to notice.

The children had eaten noisily, sparring through their
own meal—the chubby-cheeked girl and a boy still in that
androgynous three-year-old stage. But they were quiet
through the grownups' meal, having settled in front of the
television for a Disney movie.

During dinner Samantha and Stan reminisced some, but
mostly the talk was of politics. Linn was more conservative than Stan, and they argued in a mild sort of way about

events in the Soviet Dis-union, as Linn called it, and in the
Muddled East. Samantha's style was to potshot at them
both, asking leading questions that kept the argument going, as if she enjoyed watching them go head-to-head.
Becca was uncomfortable and couldn't have said why,
though she guessed it had more to do with style than sub-
stance.

In the middle of dessert—a truly delicious crème brûlee
(something else Samantha was good at)—with both children draped over her begging for bites, Samantha said suddenly, "Of course poor Becca is waiting for answers to all
her questions. Otherwise it's a long way to come for a
meal. Let me put the monsters to bed, Stan, and you explain."

Becca turned sharply to Stan and he put his hands up in
a gesture of surrender. "What she means is that she and
Linn have invited some of the Oswego people who were
living around here in the forties and may be able to remember stuff. Linn's been on the board of the Fort museum and Sam did some illustrations for their brochures.
So they are pretty linked in with what went on back then."

Just then the bell rang and Linn got up. He opened the
door and ushered in two men and a woman, all in their
sixties or seventies.

Linn introduced them around and settled everyone in the
living room with coffee.

The tired-looking man, with a shock of white hair and
pouched blue eyes that had been piercing before exhaus-
tion paled them down to a watery color, was Randolph
Feist. He had been an Oswego high school teacher.

The woman, Marge Pierce, smoothed her hennaed hair
down, not once but twice, before sitting. She comman-
deered the overstuffed chair, offering as her reason for
doing, "Lived here all my life." Her ankles were puffy and
her feet seemed shoved into the tiny shoes.

Becca's attention was taken most by Harvey Goldman.
Small, compact as a runner, he had a face the shade of old
parchment that had been written over and scraped down

too many times. What had been written, she guessed, had not always been pleasant.

They passed a few minutes in small talk—the weather, the drive up, how Oswego had changed over the years. "Not for the best," Marge offered. She repeated it immediately. "Not for the best."

In the middle of Marge's second opinion on the state of Oswego affairs, Becca suddenly got up and went into the hallway where she had left the rosewood box. She brought it back into the living room, cradling it in her arms as if it were a newborn.

Stan was just finishing a summation of their reasons for visiting, when Becca returned, saying, "So if we could know something of your . . . involvement . . . with the refugees and the Haven. And perhaps if you could look at some photographs."

Randolph cleared his throat. "I was one of the teachers who took the high school students out to the camp at open house . . ."

"Not so open for us," Harvey interrupted.

"You see," Randolph continued as if Harvey hadn't spoken, "there'd been these rumors. . . ." He paused.

"What kind of rumors?" asked Becca.

"Well, silly rumors, really. But that the refugees—and there were nearly a thousand of them—were living high at the taxpayers' expense. And this, of course, after all we had been put through because of the war. The boys and girls had talked of nothing else for days, which meant of course that their parents were saying the same things—or worse—at home. High schoolers are like that, repeating their parents' arguments as if they are their own. So Ralph . . ."

"Mr. Cornell," Marge put in, touching her hair again, "the principal. I was one of those kids. And you should have *heard* some of the things they were saying!"

". . . so Ralph insisted that the students go to see for themselves. And one look at those bare barracks and the barbed wire . . ."

"Barbs!" Becca whispered.

"Barbed wire?" Stan asked. "But these were refugees, not prisoners."

"Barbed wire!" Harvey said emphatically. "And this, mind you, while the German POWs in other parts of the country were given weekend passes!"

"But after we saw," Marge said, almost quivering with eagerness, "some of us came every afternoon after school to bring candy and stuff."

Harvey sniffed. "And you shoved it through the wire as if we were animals in a zoo." Clearly it was an old argument.

"Now, Harvey, you know the refugee children got to go to school once things settled down a bit," Randolph said. "And it was a *long* time ago."

"Time does not excuse conscience," Harvey said shortly. "Time does not erase this." He unbuttoned his left sleeve and shoved the material back up his arm. Then he held out the arm for them all the see. There was a number tattooed in faded blue.

"No," Stan put in smoothly, "time may heal wounds, but it does not erase the scars."

Harvey rolled the sleeve back down and silently rebuttoned the cuff. Marge looked down at her feet, and crossed and recrossed her puffy ankles three times as if that were some sort of a charm. Randolph looked entreatingly at Becca.

"What else do you want to know?" he asked. "We have a museum now. The Safe Haven Museum. And the Gruber book. It's called *Haven*. Have you seen it?"

"Mr. Feist," Becca said, "I never even *heard* of Fort Oswego before a few days ago. When my grandmother died, we found this box among her things. There were newspaper clippings from the *Palladium Times* and some old photos. I'm just trying to track down her past. She may have been in the refugee camp. At least she has some papers that suggest that." Becca was careful not to say anything about the fairy tale.

"What name?" Harvey asked.

"Gitl. Gitl Mandlestein. Or Dawna Stein. Or Genevieve. She seems to have had a number of names," Becca said.

"Gitl. Gitl." Harvey closed his eyes and his fingers rubbed his left arm, as if the number under the shirt could be read like braille. He shook his head slowly. "Dawna. Genevieve."

"Can I show you the photos?" Becca asked, her voice almost a whisper.

"Done!" Coming into the room with a burst of energy, Samantha's cheery voice seemed to energize them all. "The monsters are down for the night. More coffee anyone?"

The cups were refilled and whatever tension had been in the room was effectively broken. Becca suspected that Samantha had planned it that way, an entrance as dramatic as any on stage. She immediately felt guilty about the thought, as if to think such a thing of Stan's old friend was a disloyalty of the worst kind. Hastily she drew out the photos and passed the first to Harvey.

He shook his head. "So long ago," he whispered. But he stared at one of the pictures, where a number of people crowded around Gemma in her sack dress. He placed his second finger, right hand, on top of one young man. Becca saw he had no nail on that finger.

"What is it, Harvey?" Samantha asked. "Are you all right?" Harvey had closed his eyes. She placed her hand over his.

"That's me," he said. "That's the only photograph, of all the ones we have in the museum, that has me in it. It makes the old nightmares real."

Becca stared at the photo in his hand. The face of the young man was hungry; he was staring yearningly at Gemma.

"And that's Księżniczka."

"What!" Becca and Stan spoke together, and Stan leaned forward as well.

"We called her that. It meant princess. Because . . ."

Suddenly he looked puzzled, as if memory—and the desire to remember—were simply not enough.

"Because she was born in a castle?" Becca asked, the words almost painful in her throat.

"A Jew born in a castle?" Harvey was momentarily nonplussed. "No—because she would have nothing to do with the rest of us. With me. As if . . ." His voice trailed off. Almost as an afterthought, he added, "It's so long ago."

"Can't you remember?" Becca begged. "Anything? Did she go to school? Did she talk about the past? Did she. . .?"

"She had a new baby but no husband and . . . That is all I remember."

"Please try, Mr. Goldman," Becca begged. "Please."

Randolph held up his hand as he must have done so often in the classroom. "Harvey's right. It's *all* so long ago. And memory is such a strange and unwieldy device. We remember *odd* things. Like the old woman who kissed the ground when she arrived."

"*You* didn't see that, Randolph," Marge interrupted. "It was in the paper."

"You're probably right," Randolph admitted. "But it *seems* as if I remember it. That's what I mean about memory. Still, I do remember the refugee children who came to school. Pathetic little things most of them, undernourished, jumpy. And how they stuck together. But so bright, even in their broken English." He smiled. "This Ruth Gruber who wrote the book, she was the one who got to pick which refugees came to the Fort, and they weren't all Jews either. Some were Catholics, who were allowed out to attend mass at my church because it was nearest the Fort. And some Protestants, too, I remember."

"From Italy we came," Harvey said. "From hot to cold. And one baby died in the crossing. *That* I remember. The mother could not cry for two days, but she could not speak either, until we passed the Statue of Liberty. Then with everyone else crying with joy she, poor thing, sobbed her sorrow."

For a moment they were all silent.

"And I remember thinking," Harvey continued, "how free we were. At last. How free. And how shocked I was when we were suddenly back behind barbed wire again. I was sure we had come all that way just to be killed in America."

"And look at you now," Marge said. "You own half of Oswego."

"I have one small shop, but I am content," Harvey said immediately. "How is that half of the city?"

"Please," Becca interrupted, not having Samantha's gift of surprise, "what about my grandmother?"

"She carried herself like a princess," said Harvey. "That I *do* remember. She was like something out of a fairy book, the fairest skin and the reddest hair, as if the war and all the horrors could not touch that beauty. You look quite a bit like her, except for the eyes. Your eyes are warm. They are here. Hers were—somewhere else. We boys were all half in love with her, I think. But she did not speak to any of us. It was as if a curse had been placed upon her."

"A curse?" Becca said.

"The Nazis were the curse," said Harvey. "They still are."

"The Nazis are all dead, Harvey," Marge said, her hands once more smoothing down her hair.

"For you they are dead," he said. "Not for me." He sighed and stood. "I must go. It is too late for an old man like me."

"I am an old man, too," Randolph said.

"But not like me," said Harvey. He winked at Becca, then took her hand. "I am glad to have met the granddaughter of Księżniczka." Smiling shyly, he kissed her hand. Then he gave Samantha a kiss on both cheeks and left.

The rest soon followed.

CHAPTER

13

"A prince came from a nearby country," said Gemma. Becca was in bed with pneumonia. Her sisters called it "Flu-monia" and tried to get it, too. But Gemma shooed them away. "You can't get out of school that easily," she said.

"Why is it always a prince who rescues her?" asked Becca.

"You watch too much television," said Gemma. "Too much Geraldo and Donahue. Too much women's rights. In the old days it was a prince."

Becca's chest and throat hurt too much to argue.

"The prince came riding by with all his troops. He saw the hedge and he tried to see over it. He tried to see under it."

"Why didn't he just uproot it?" Becca asked, the fever making her cranky.

"It would have torn his poor hands to shreds," Gemma said. She took a cool cloth and wiped Becca's face with it slowly, and hummed a bit through her nose. "Just then a peasant came by and saw him trying to see over and trying to see under. 'Better not,' the peasant said. 'Whoever goes in doesn't come out.' "

"The prince turned to the peasant. 'And how do you know?' The peasant smiled. He had only a few teeth. 'We peasants always know this sort of thing.' " Gemma paused and put the cloth into the basin on the dresser, then turned back to Becca who was almost asleep. " 'But do you know courage?' asked the prince. And so saying, he put his right hand into the thorns."

Becca shivered. This was the part of the story she loved the best, better than the kiss, better than the wedding, better than the curse. She didn't know why. Having pneumonia meant that once she started shivering, she could not stop. Gemma pulled the covers up around her and then lay down by her side, giving her extra warmth. Becca was asleep before the story ended.

CHAPTER
14

The museum had been an anticlimax. There were no pictures in which Gemma appeared, though there were photos of hundreds of women dressed in sack dresses. And as Harvey Goldman had said, none in which he could be identified either. The rest of the exhibits were interesting and depressing.

"Like most histories," Samantha commented. As a member of the board, Linn had been able to get them in early Sunday morning and, with the place to themselves, they were loud in their commentaries.

"Like most morgues," Stan said. "It's why I prefer current events."

Becca looked up sharply from the picture she'd been examining. It was as if Stan had suddenly explained himself to her. "Find out what the past has to say, and then move on?" she asked.

"Yes!" He grinned at her.

"Well, this past doesn't seem to say anything more about my grandmother except she was here."

"Then where was she before she got *here*?" asked Samantha.

"The sixty-four-million-dollar question," said Stan.

"That used to be the sixty-four-dollar question," Linn said.

"Inflation!" Stan and Samantha and Becca all said together. They were still laughing about it when they locked the door to the Safe Haven Museum behind them.

The ride home seemed to go too fast. Becca and Stan sang old songs and told family stories, and even discussed a couple of pieces that Becca wanted to write for the *Advocate*. Two of them Stan vetoed but the third made him turn his head towards her. "That *interests* me," he said.

"She sets the hook," Becca said, smiling.

She slept all the way from Albany, apologizing profusely when, upon waking with a start, she saw they were just coming off Route 91 into Hatfield.

"Gave me time to think," Stan said. "I find it hard to think around you."

Becca decided not to ask what that meant. It might mean nothing. It might mean something. Either way she foresaw problems.

"What did you think about?" she asked.

"About the princess. And where she was before she got to the Fort. I'd like to look at those papers again."

"Tomorrow," Becca said.

"Lunch," Stan agreed.

He let her off at the house but didn't come in. He didn't try to kiss her, but he didn't shake her hand, either. Becca thought that meant they hadn't been on a date, but were closer than just colleagues. She'd think about it later, when Stan wasn't around.

Her parents were asleep when she got in, so she spread all the papers and photos once more over the dining room table. Gemma's face stared up at her, with Harvey Goldman's hungry face behind.

"Oh, Gemma," Becca whispered, "what are you looking at? The past? Or the present? Or maybe seeing into the future?"

A hand on her shoulder startled her. "Glad you got back safely, sweetheart." It was her father in his pajamas. "Learn anything new?"

"Gemma *was* at Fort Oswego. There was a man there who remembered her. Remembered her as The Princess."

"And was she?"

"Oh, Daddy!" She smiled.

"Never heard of Jewish American Princesses?" he asked.

"Oh, Daddy!" she repeated.

He kissed the top of her head. "We are so lucky, you know," he said. "Whatever Gemma went through and remembered, or didn't remember, *we* are so lucky."

"I know, Daddy," Becca said softly. "Listening to Harvey Goldman and seeing all those photographs and the number on his arm and . . . Daddy!"

"What?"

"Gemma didn't *have* any number. So she couldn't have been in a camp. So what kind of refugee was she?"

"Not all the camps burned numbers into the prisoners' arms, Becca," he said. "Not all of them kept their prisoners long enough."

"How do you know that?"

He spoke into her hair. "I read more than medical journals, my sweet. Go to bed."

She stood up, turned, and hugged him, then dutifully went up to her room. She didn't hear him on the stairs and pictured him sitting at the dining room table turning the pieces of paper over and over as if, by touching them, he could solve the puzzle.

Stan and she sat on a blanket by the waterfall and shuffled through the papers once again. The one Stan finally stopped at was the biographical data form.

"This," he said, pointing to the line that was crossed out.

Squinting in the sun, Becca read: WHAT WAS YOUR

LAST PERMANENT ADDRESS. "Can't read it," she said.

"It's our only clue, Becca. We're going to *have* to read it. Let's see if we can enlarge it." He stood and pulled her to her feet. "Come on."

Hastily Becca picked up the yogurt containers and Stan's grinder wrapper while he gathered Gemma's papers. They left the blanket for later.

At the Xerox machine, Stan enlarged the paper three times until the scratched-out portion was large enough to read.

"That's a K," he said.

"K-E-L . . . *Kelm*, something?" Becca asked.

"Looks more like *Kulm* something," Stan said.

"I think you're right. *Kulm* . . . and maybe *hef* or *hof*. There's that slash through it, though, so I can't tell if it's an *e* or an *o*. Sound German to you? Or middle European?"

"Polish," Stan said, running his fingers through his hair. "Don't forget that princess stuff. That was Polish. She'd lived in Poland at some point. My guess is she came from there."

"Or came through it."

"Good point."

"So. . . . ?"

"So get on with it. Check the atlas, call the university and . . ." He grinned.

"What about my work? I've got a couple of stories to do and—"

"*This* is going to make one hell of an article," Stan said. "I can feel it." He turned abruptly and walked back into his office, shutting the door with such finality, it felt like punctuation.

Becca stared for a long moment at the closed door, trying to imagine what Stan was doing behind it: sitting at his desk with his feet up, shooting rubber bands at the picture of George Bush in a golf cart; doodling on a paper with those blank-faced monks in robes that he always drew during story conferences; or making phone calls to old girlfriends. None of it seemed likely. Or real. What seemed real was the paper in Becca's hand and she stared down at it, and at the word—*Kulmhef* or *Kulmhof* or whatever—that had been scratched out by her grandmother in anger or horror or grief so many years before.

She went over to the atlas and opened it to the Ks. Leaning over the high desk and using the magnifying glass attached by a red string, she found the right place.

"Kulm, North Dakota," she read aloud, shaking her head. *"Sure!"* She read further. "Kulm in Switzerland, two different cantons. Kulmain and Kulmbach, both West Germany—possible. Kulmasa, Ghana, definitely not." She wrote down the two possibles and, at the last minute, wrote in the Swiss towns as well. Then she slammed the book shut.

"Becca, phone!" someone called out.

Taking the piece of paper with her, she returned to her desk. The call had to do with an old story and she fielded the questions deftly, all the while underlining the West German town names over and over. By the time she hung up, she had gone through the paper with the pen point in two places.

But something about the names bothered her, and she shook her head back and forth as if that could dislodge the problem. Before she could puzzle it through, Stan's door opened and he leaned very casually against the jamb. "Anything?"

"One North Dakota and one Ghana, two Swiss and two West German. None of them exactly *Kulmhof* or *Kulmhef.*"

"Hmmm." He took off his wire-rimmed glasses and polished them on the front of his shirt. He didn't speak again until he'd replaced them on his nose. "Maybe we should call Samantha's friend and ask."

"Which one?"

He cocked his head to one side and twisted his mouth, as if to say: *You kidding?*

"Harvey Goldman," she answered herself.

"I have his card here somewhere," Stan said, pulling out a handful of change, car keys, and about ten business cards from his pocket. "He gave it to me before he left. 'In case you need to know anything,' he said. 'Or want to buy a shirt.'" He sorted through the cards quickly. "Here: Harvey's Haberdasher's." He chuckled. "Can't believe anyone would still call a store that!"

Becca took the card from him, careful not to touch his hand, and went back to her desk. She sat down slowly and pushed each button on the phone as if it were made of glass. For some reason she was suddenly reluctant to call, not at all the way she usually felt when moving ahead on a story.

The phone rang twice, then was answered by a cheery young female voice. "Harvey's. Can I help you?"

"May I speak to Harvey Goldman, please. It's not business, so I can wait," Becca said.

"Grandpa!" the girl yelled, her voice only slightly removed from the phone.

Becca heard a slight shuffling, then an admonishing, "Don't yell, Mirra," and finally a clear and recognizable voice said, "Harvey Goldman here."

"Mr. Goldman, this is Becca Berlin, the woman tracing her grandmother. We met Saturday at Samantha and Linn's house."

"Yes, yes, I remember. I am very good with names," Harvey said. "Except, of course, your grandmother's." He chuckled.

Becca's hand felt sweaty on the phone. "I . . . we . . . that is, Stan and I enlarged one of the forms on the copier and we discovered something we thought you might be able to help us with."

"Anything," Harvey said. "Oh excuse me a minute. Mirra, please help that gentleman. Yes, you were saying, Becca?"

"There is a line on one of the forms—'what was your last permanent address.' And the answer's been crossed out, but we were able to make out something, only I can't find any reference to it in our atlas. At least not exactly. And Stan thought you might recognize it."

"I will try. What does it say?"

Becca took a deep breath. "It says, well it looks like . . . *Kulmhof* or *Kelmhof* or maybe *hef*." She stopped and waited.

There was no sound except a kind of heavy breathing on the other end of the phone.

"Mr. Goldman? Harvey?"

Nothing.

"Are you there? Did I pronounce it wrong?" Becca asked.

"Kulmhof!" he said. "My God!"

"Is it somewhere?" Becca asked, her voice a harsh whisper.

"In the darkest regions of hell."

"I beg your pardon?"

"You asked where it was, Rebecca, and I answered you. Kulmhof. It was not even a concentration camp. It was simply a place of . . . extermination."

"Then my grandmother was there?"

"That is not possible, my dear," Harvey said, his voice suddenly very old. "No woman ever escaped Kulmhof alive."

CHAPTER

15

"As the prince's hand came near the thorns, all the bones of the many princes who had been there before him rose up from the thorn bush singing."

"What did they sing, Gemma?" Becca asked. She'd never asked the question before. She and Gemma were part of a class trip and the other children on the bus were busy throwing things and punching one another on the arms. Only Gemma and Becca—and a boy named Barney who had something wrong with his hands and so no one else would play with him—were listening to the story.

For a moment Gemma looked stumped. Then she sang:

> "Tsvantsik mayl bin ikh gelofn
> Hob ikh a shtibl ongetrofn.
> Balebos! Git mir a shtikl broyt;
> Zet mayn ponem, vi bleykh un toyt.
> Ikh hob zikh gevashn un gebentsht,
> Iz arayn a khapermentsh. . . ."

Her voice trailed off and she looked out the window.

The words of the song were so harsh and ugly, Becca

_was afraid to ask what they meant. But Barney had no
such fears._

"Mrs. Stein," he said, "is that silliness? Or what?"

Gemma pulled her eyes from the window and stared directly at Barney. "Or what."

"Gemma, finish the story," Becca begged, suddenly
afraid. "The real story."

"I don't like stories I don't understand," Barney said.
"My dad always says to ask if you don't understand something." Barney was a great asker in school.

"So—what do you want to know, Barney?" Gemma
said.

"What those funny words mean. Do they mean anything?"

Gemma nodded and looked out the window again.

By this time Becca was caught up in the contest of wills.
"What do they mean? Tell us."

Gemma sighed. "It's an old song. An old song for an
old story. They say:

> I ran and ran for twenty miles
> Until I came upon a house.
> Sir! Give me a piece of bread;
> Look at me: I'm pale and dead.
> I had already washed and said the blessing
> When in walked the khapermentshn . . ."

"What are khaper . . ." Barney began.

". . . mentshn?" Becca finished.

"Kidnappers," Gemma explained curtly.

"Kidnappers?" There was outrage in Barney's voice.
"There aren't any kidnappers in Sleeping Beauty."

Gemma looked at him fiercely. "What do you know
about stories? What do you know about Briar Rose?"

Under her withering gaze, he turned around in his seat
and did not look back again. Gemma did not say another
word the rest of the trip home.

CHAPTER

16

"And he said Kulmhof was one of the first of the extermination camps to open," Becca said that night at dinner, her plate of food lying untouched in front of her.

"Becca, eat," her mother said, not touching any of her own food.

"When had it opened?" her father asked.

"Sometime in 'forty-one, he said. His voice was real shaky when he talked about it, but not like he was scared, more like he was angry. Furious. Furious and unable to do anything about that fury," Becca said. She looked down at the cold food. Normally beef in beer sauce was a favorite of hers. "Jews and Gypsies, he said, were the main victims at Kulmhof."

Dr. Berlin cleared his throat. "It was an awful long time ago," he said. "We can't do anything about . . ."

"This was *Gemma*," Becca said.

Her mother reached out and touched her; it was as if her hand were hot as a brand. Becca could feel it sear right down to the bone. "But Mr. Goldman said no woman had escaped from there so it couldn't have been Gemma."

Becca ignored the burning hand. "He said Kulmhof was about fifty miles northwest of Lodz in Poland."

"Poland. . . ." Mrs. Berlin said.

"And here we are in a Polish farm community," Dr. Berlin said. "No wonder Gemma chose it."

"But no woman ever escaped from Kulmhof," Becca whispered. "And why would she choose to live among Poles here in America, if . . ."

"It was probably her family that died in Kulmhof, then," said Dr. Berlin. "And maybe she thought by living amongst Poles here, she might somehow get word of them."

"What family?" Mrs. Berlin asked. "I always thought *I* was all her family."

"Until *we* came along," Becca added, remembering how often Gemma had said, *"This is my family,"* loudly and with such outlandish pride at each graduation or Honor Society induction or ball game that they had all been embarrassed.

"It explains a lot," Dr. Berlin said, pushing his plate away with both hands.

"It doesn't explain anything," Mrs. Berlin said quietly, almost in a whisper.

Becca waited a moment for the silence that followed to be broken. Then she said, matching her mother whisper for whisper, "There *is* a place where it could all be explained."

"No!" Dr. Berlin said, shaking his head. "No!"

"At Kulmhof—if it still exists. Fifty miles from Lodz." She pronounced it carefully, remembering Goldman's voice as he said it, the horrible hush.

"Not possible," her father said.

"I promised Gemma. I swore I would find our inheritance."

"A concentration camp is not an inheritance."

"A burden?" Mrs. Berlin said quietly. "A family secret?"

"I promised," Becca repeated. "I swore." She stood and smiled grimly. "It's a kind of fairy tale, isn't it."

Her parents began to argue even before she left the room.

She thought about it as she lay in bed and her dreams were filled with images of the camps, gleaned from many horror movies: the scarecrow men, their ribs protruding like hideous maps; the piles of bodies in the mass graves all grown together as if in a garden of death; children with eyes like devalued coins, caught behind the wire barbs.

She got up early, exhausted, and was in the office even before Stan; she was tracing several possible routes to Lodz in the atlas when he walked in.

He didn't even say hello, just came and stared over her shoulder as her finger moved across the Polish border towards Lodz one more time.

"A sudden passion for *galumpkis*?" he asked.

She smiled briefly, then moved away as if his shadow on hers was an uncomfortable burden. Turning instead to look directly and seriously at him, she said, "I called Goldman."

"I thought you might." He did not pursue it, waiting patiently for her.

"He said Kulmhof was an extermination camp."

"Jesus!"

"And that no woman ever got out of there alive."

"Hmmmm." His hand went up to his hair automatically and he scratched at his scalp as he spoke. "So—she wasn't there. Or maybe she had family there or . . ."

"I'm going," Becca said shortly.

"Of course you are." He smiled. "Wish I could come, too." Then he went into his office and closed the door.

Becca turned back to the map. "Of course I am," she muttered. If it hadn't been settled before, it was now. All she had to do was find out how to get there, how much it would cost, and someone to do her translating. The only Polish she knew was limited to food—and the name of a single camp.

* * *

Her University of Massachusetts contacts pointed her to the Slavic Department. A professor there told her to check on a book called the *Atlas Samochodowy Polski*, which she got down correctly after three wrong tries.

"I'll have it transferred downstairs to the reference librarian's desk," he said. "If you trace the route, check on road number eighty-one. I'm pretty sure that's the right one. It goes out of Warsaw, to Plock, then to Torun, then to Bydgozcz . . ."

Becca took the names down phonetically, then asked him to spell them correctly.

"Chelmno is a half hour from there by car."

"I'm sorry," Becca said, "but the name is Kulmhof."

"That's the German name," the professor told her. "When the Germans took over, they called it Kulmhof. Its Polish name—what it's called now—is Chelmno."

"Chelmno," Becca repeated. It made her shiver in a way that she hadn't before, as if the word itself had been imprinted in her genes. "Chelmno."

"You will pass through many lovely places," the professor was saying. "These are old cities, not like American cities, and the land around them is mainly flat and green. One of the cities . . ."

She stopped listening. All the pictures she had seen of concentration camps came back to her in a rush; her dreams of last night seemed as clear as if she were staring directly at the past.

". . . to the thirteenth century," he was saying.

"Thank you very much, Professor Radziwicz," Becca said. "Can I call you again if necessary?"

"My pleasure," he said. "And you may want to check also with the Polish Jewish program at the University of Connecticut in Storrs. It is connected, I believe, with the Polish Jewish Institute in Cracow."

She took down all the information, thanked him twice more, and hung up. The paper on which she'd taken notes was full, and on the sides, like some sort of horrible marginalia, were rows and rows of swastikas. She had no memory of drawing them.

Standing, she thought *Why am I doing this*? And answered herself aloud, "For Gemma." But that wasn't right and she knew it. "For all of us." She shook her head. Then she walked into Stan's office without knocking.

He glanced up. The light glinting off his glasses blocked his eyes and for a moment he looked blind.

She sat in the chair reserved for visitors. "Tell me again why you searched for your birth mother."

"Because I had to. Blood calling to blood, and all that." He leaned forward across the desk and stared at her. Without the light on the glass, his eyes were so blue she felt cut by them, as if they were ice.

"That's not it," she said.

"Because I was so damned curious, I had to find out or die," he said.

"That's closer."

There was a hush between them that stretched out until it was simply a thin line. Becca felt herself poised to walk across it carefully like a circus acrobat.

"Because . . ." he whispered, "what's past is prologue."

"Shakespeare," she said, quietly. "I forget just where."

"The Tempest," he countered. "But it's true."

"You didn't answer me truly."

"I don't know—truly. I only knew I had to do it."

"Okay." She stood. "I am going to want my two weeks vacation early, and an extra week without pay."

"Will you write the story?"

"If there is one."

"Happy ending or no?" He was serious.

She attempted a smile. "Fairy tales always have a happy ending."

He leaned back in his chair. "That depends."

"On what?"

"On whether you are Rumplestiltskin or the Queen."

* * *

It took longer than she thought to set the trip up. The pass-port and visa alone was a three week project. The Polish Embassy in Washington, D.C., was helpful, but the Boston passport office was not. The Polish Tourist Office in New York gave her car information. "You can rent through us," the woman had said, her voice light and fruity, with just a touch of an accent. "A Fiat Uno for six days, less than two hundred dollars, and drive from Warsaw. It only takes four hours."

Becca hung up, having arranged for the Fiat, a variety of maps, and information about restaurants and hotels.

On her father's suggestion, she contacted the Polish Jewish program at Storrs for a possible translator and they promised a student would meet her at the plane. For a small fee (and several pairs of blue jeans, size twelve, the woman suggested), she would be in the capable hands of Magda Bronski.

"Sounds like a novelist's idea of a Polish woman some-what below a countess," Becca had said.

The woman at Storrs had chuckled, her laugh over the phone comforting. "Mother Jewish, father not. The girl is rediscovering her roots. A lot of them are these days."

"Me, too," Becca said.

"In Chelmno?" The woman's voice was suddenly dark. "All the roots there were severed."

Becca told Stan of the conversation, but not her parents. He only shook his head and asked her for a due date on another story. It was as if his interest in her trip was purely professional now. Becca felt that withdrawal as a deep loss, and she couldn't say why.

Clearly her father was still troubled about the trip because within days Becca got three phone calls, one from Sylvia, two from Shana.

"This is crazy," Syl shouted into the phone.

"I made a promise," Becca said.

"Deathbed promises don't count."

"If deathbed promises don't count," Becca countered, "what kind of promises do?"

Syl made a list of promises, including peace treaties, marriage vows, and New Year's resolutions. "And all of them are broken regularly," she finished.

"This was a promise to Gemma," said Becca, hanging up and feeling—as she usually did after arguing with one of her sisters—morally oppressed.

Shana called not long after, and Becca was careful not to discuss her trip in terms of the promise to Gemma. "I didn't take a vacation last year because of Gemma and so I have two weeks coming. And by taking a third on my own, I'll get to see a lot of Eastern Europe."

"But Daddy says you're going to a concentration camp. What kind of vacation is that?"

"An *extermination* camp, but I'll see churches and cathedrals and lots of other historical things." She shuffled quickly through the many notes she had taken, came across the paper with the swastikas. "I'll see some of the cities on the Vistula. In fact, one of the experts I talked to says there is a thirteenth-century cathedral there that has been designated by the U.N. as one of the world's most architecturally important monuments."

"A vacation expert told you this?" Shana wasn't convinced.

"Who else?" She hated to lie but she hated arguments even more.

Shana hung up slightly mollified and called back less than an hour later. "You're going because of that promise!" she said. "Not a cathedral."

"You've been talking to Syl."

"Well, you're not to go. Especially with the political situation there. It's liable to blow up any minute."

"That's the Soviet republics," Becca explained carefully. "That's Yugoslavia. Not Poland. Poland is quite stable at the moment."

"At the moment. . . ."

It took another ten minutes before Shana would let her

go, and the whole evening had tired Becca out. She went to bed and finished only a few pages of McKinley's *Beauty*, a book she reread whenever she felt troubled.

Though she'd set June first as a possible travel date, she had to be satisfied with June fifteenth.

"Best laid plans and all that," she explained to Stan. "Slow passport, slow visa, and Baroness Magda's availability."

"A real baroness?"

"Am I a real granddaughter of a princess?"

"I don't know—are you?"

"Sometime after June fifteenth I might actually know." She smiled slightly, but he didn't smile back. "Look, don't tell anyone here what I am doing in Poland."

"It's your story, Becca," he said. "You alone can break the spell."

"Spell?"

"That's what I finally decided. You asked why I had to look for my birth mother and I put you off with quick answers. But in the end, all I could think of—and believe me, I have been thinking about it a lot these past weeks—is that I alone could break the spell. It wasn't so much *finding* her as *looking* for her. And only I could do it." This time he smiled—grinned, actually—and held out his hand.

She took it and felt real pleasure when he squeezed it.

"As far as the office is concerned, it's a vacation mixed with a bit of reporting. When you come back, you can decide how much to tell and who to tell, but . . ." His grin turned wicked, one corner tilting up higher than the other.

"But you want the story."

"In writing."

"It begins Once Upon a Time."

His grin faded. "Don't count on Happy Ever After. This is the real world."

"I won't. How happy can it be? Gemma's dead, after all." She turned away and went back to her desk, packing up everything she would need for the trip. Stan watched her go from the door.

She waved good-bye to the other reporters and Jim in production came up to give her a big hug. As she went through the waiting room, Merelle was just bending over to pick up her pocketbook.

"Oh, bye, Becca. I hear you're going off to Poland. You might want to be sure and look at the paper cut-outs. My friend Jannie just went last year and she stayed with her great aunt and uncle. Had never met them before. They took her to this open air market where there were these paper things."

"I'm going on a story actually," Becca said.

"What kind of story?"

"A fairy story," Becca said.

"Gay rights?" Merelle looked puzzled.

"Sleeping Beauty."

"You are *such* a kidder, Becca," Merelle said. "Have a good trip. Break a leg."

Becca smiled, nodded her head, and left. "Break a spell would be more appropriate," she said aloud as she walked down the road.

CHAPTER

17

"The prince sang, too, and as he added his voice to theirs, it was as if he witnessed all their deaths in the thorns. It was as if he had knowledge of all their lives, past and present and future."

"How can they have any future lives if they're dead?" Syl had asked, finally. It was a question the girls had puzzled over in the family room, as they played with their dollhouse. Shana had wondered first and both the older girls had wanted Becca to ask. But she had refused. So Syl, being braver that year, had done what they had all wanted.

"How?" Syl asked again.

Gemma looked over her half glasses and said, "The future is when people talk about the past. So if the prince knows all their past lives and tells all the people who are still to come, then the princes live again and into the future."

"Oh," said Syl, as if she understood, but she hadn't. She said that later, when Gemma had finished the story and the girls were once again playing at dolls. "I didn't understand at all."

"I didn't either," Shana said, marching the mommy doll from the living room to the kitchen.

"Didn't either," said Becca, even though she did. But she had long ago learned it was best not to contradict her sisters. They just got mad. She put the baby doll into its cradle and went out of the room to their real kitchen where Gemma was making a cake.

"I understand," she said to Gemma.

"You always understand," Gemma said, handing her the icing bowl to lick. Becca preferred licking the cake dough bowl, but it was already sitting in the sink with soapy water.

"Always," Becca agreed, though she wondered if this were really true.

CHAPTER

18

The plane was already an hour late and Becca was long past trying to sleep. The pilot had twice promised they would make up the time, once when they boarded in Milan and once somewhere over the Italian border. He had not promised since.

Becca unfastened her seatbelt and, careful not to disturb her seatmate, bent over to get her pocketbook from the floor. Unzipping it, she took out her passport and the envelope with the photos of Gemma. Then she pulled down the seat tray and spread the photos out, placing the opened passport next to them. It was something she had done a hundred times since having her picture taken. Though Gemma's photos were in black-and-white, grainy reminders of time passing, and hers was brilliant—and wrong—in its coloring, the two women could have been one. The same surprised eyes, the same strong mouth, the same broad forehead, the same heart-shaped face narrowing to a chin that missed being pointed by a small cleft. No one had ever commented on how much they looked alike, she and Gemma, except of course for the red hair. But then, no one had ever seen the pictures of Gemma as a young woman before. Still, the resemblance startled Becca anew.

"How many more surprises, Gemma?" Becca whispered. The sound of her voice, even pitched so low, woke her seatmate. A chatty woman with Polish cousins, she started in on her bland reminiscences even before the sleep was fully cast from her eyes.

Becca listened only half-heartedly; the woman tended to repeat herself endlessly. That was the third time she was telling this particular story. Putting away the photos, Becca kept the passport out a minute longer, opening and closing it. It was so fresh, so new. Soon it would have its first stamps. Polish stamps. Border stamps. Almost a violation, though welcome. Gemma, she remembered suddenly, had had no passport, not in her bank box, not in the rose box. In fact Gemma had often boasted how she was perfectly happy in America and had no intention of ever crossing another border. Most probably, Becca thought, she never had a passport; the woman at Storrs said the majority of the refugees were considered displaced persons who had gotten their visas through American consulates. "Someone running desperately in a war," she'd said, "rarely stops to find the proper papers."

Becca thought about her grandmother, about the war she had been running from when she was close to Becca's age. Then she put the passport back in her pocketbook, zipping it closed with a sound that was both rude and funny. Smiling, she turned to her seatmate.

"I've never been to Poland," she said, cutting into the woman's monologue.

"Well, I have, my dear," the woman answered. "Third time. And my cousins . . ."

"I've never actually been *anywhere* before."

"Sort of a Sleeping Beauty, are you?"

Becca started laughing and could not stop. The woman looked shocked and after a moment rang the call button. A stewardess, fearing she had a hysteric on her hands, came running with a glass of cold water.

* * *

Having nothing to declare but the blue jeans for Magda ("Not even a set of cousins," she thought to herself, but knew better than to make jokes with customs officers), Becca got through the long line with relatively little fuss. There was no size twelve student waiting for her, so she stopped for a moment to glance around. The airport was decidedly low-tech, not like an American airport at all. Three young women in embroidered skirts and dirndls were the only spot of color. They were holding up a sign in English: "Welkom Aunt Anna and Uncle Stosh." She resisted the urge to copyedit it.

When no one tapped her on the shoulder, she perched on top of her suitcase and waited, lulled by the buzz of voices. It occurred to her that if Magda size twelve didn't show up, she might have some serious problems making herself understood, the Polish phrasebook in her coat pocket notwithstanding. But within five minutes—a very long five minutes—a broad-faced, blonde young woman, much smaller than a size twelve, stopped before her and asked: "Miss Berlin?"

"Magda?"

"I am so pleased to make your acquaintance." Magda held out a hand whose grip turned out to be firm and familiar. "There was much cars today."

"Traffic?"

"Yes, traffic. I think my English will much improve for the next three weeks."

Becca smiled. *"Over."*

Magda looked puzzled. "Over?"

"Over the next three weeks." Becca picked up her suitcase. "Maybe I can learn a little Polish, too."

"All things are possible." Magda's face was sunny and open, as if deceit were a foreign commodity. Her eyebrows worked independently of one another, which gave her the look of a slightly demented dove. Becca decided she liked that.

"What do we do first?"

"You must have changed money. And then we go to my aunt's apartment where we will spend the night. It is too late to go off and without good plans. Tomorrow we get the automobile."

"We would say *car*."

"Yes, the car. And I will show you tonight some of Warsaw, if you are not too tired. It is a wonderful city for tourists and has been much rebuilded since the war." During this little speech, Magda had carefully guided them to a kiosk where money was exchanged. "How much would you like changed?"

Becca took out a packet of traveler's checks. "Would two hundred do?"

Magda grinned and her right and left eyebrows did their little independent dances. "It will do very well, though you must keep also dollars ready. People like dollars very much. Do not say I told you this." She turned and spoke quickly in Polish to the woman behind the counter.

The woman leaned forward and said in heavily accented English, "Do not trouble. I am speaking your language. Sign the checks, and I give you zlotys. It is forbidden to take zlotys out of country. All must be spent here."

"You see—many speak English here in Poland," Magda said expansively. "Perhaps you will have no need of me."

"I will have much need of you," Becca said. "Especially once we go out into the countryside."

"Especially then," Magda agreed cheerfully.

They left the airport and got a taxi. "Just give him dollars," Magda advised. "That is the way to make it very inex . . . how do you say, cheap?"

An hour later, with Magda pointing out the sights— "That is the River Vistula, and there is the Old Town, perhaps we will look there, and that dome like an onion is St. John's and where the Jesuits—is that right, Jesuit?—yes, church. And—" They arrived at their destination.

Becca gave the driver one-dollar bills, counting them out into his open hand, his round, ruddy face beaming with delight.

"Too much, too much," Magda said loudly, but Becca kept up the count. Finally Magda put her hand palm down over the driver's at seven dollars. "*Wystarczy!* Enough!" she said roughly to him and he made a face back at her.

They got out and Becca was delighted to see that they were in a much older part of the city.

"Auntie lives there." Magda pointed to a series of low buildings.

"Can I pick her up a present of some kind?" Becca asked. "That is a custom in America. When you stay at someone's house . . ."

"She would love a bottle of good slivovitz," Magda said. "There is a store over there." She pointed across the street. "It is too expensive for her that often."

They bought the bottle with an awful lot of zlotys, and went on to the building that Magda had originally pointed to. Auntie lived on the fourth floor, up steep, uneven stairs. It took both of them carrying the suitcase to manage it.

"Why did you bring such a heavy case?" Magda asked, as they rounded the third floor.

"I *am* staying three weeks," Becca said, the stairs making her momentarily cranky. But she was suddenly embarrassed by all the clothing she had packed. An athletic duffel with fewer things would have made much more sense.

Auntie proved to be a greyer and wider version of Magda, as ebullient and welcoming. The slivovitz was a great hit, though Auntie Wanda insisted they all have a drink to celebrate Becca's arrival. Not being much of a drinker, Becca choked on the strong liquor, much to the amusement of Magda and her aunt.

Becca unpacked in the tiny room she was sharing with Magda only to the extent of hanging up her skirts and one dress. She pulled out the blue jeans and brought them back into the room that served as a living room, dining room, kitchen, and—she suspected—Auntie's bedroom as well. "These are for you," she said, handing them to Magda. "Though I was told size twelve and they are probably much too large. You can't be more than a size six."

"Oh, they are much in appreciation," Magda said.

"Appreciated," Becca corrected.

"That, too. I can sell them on the black market and Auntie and I will have a wonderful holiday." She said it with no embarrassment whatsoever. "She has raised me since my parents are gone. I can do not enough for her."

Becca nodded.

"Now, if you are not too tired, I will show you my city." Magda's face was so pleased-looking, Becca could not resist.

"I am not too tired," she said. "Besides, I will sleep very well tonight."

"Very well indeed," Auntie Wanda put in. "My Magda does no snoring."

Magda's city was a combination of very tall, new skyscrapers, some war ruins, and a bustling Old Town along the royal route. Magda insisted they had to go to the Royal Castle, now a treasury of art and relics. King Sigismund Vasa the Third looked down from his high column in the square. It was all so European, so unlike America, that Becca forgot how tired she was and managed to enjoy it all.

Her favorite place, though, was the summer palace of the last Polish king. Sitting on an escarpment overlooking the Vistula, with classic parks around it, the palace was just right for a fairy tale.

"I wonder," Becca said aloud, "if my grandmother's palace was like this?"

"Your grandmother had a palace?" Magda asked.

"So she said. Or at least, she said she *lived* in a palace. I promised her I'd come back and find it."

"*We* will find it," Magda said, right eyebrow arching like a bow while the left flattened momentarily. She held out her hand.

Becca took her hand. "We will," she said, and for the first time believed it.

CHAPTER

19

"And the thorns parted before him." The simple statement was always accompanied in Gemma's telling by a moment of silence from all her listeners.

Only once had Becca broken that silence early. She had had to go to the bathroom, quite desperately, yet didn't want to leave, afraid Gemma would finish the story without her. She knew the story by heart, but she didn't want to miss it. There was always the possibility that this time something new would happen.

"And the thorns parted before him," Gemma said.

On the sofa, the three girls breathed a deep, urgent breath.

"Hurry, Gemma," Becca said.

Gemma looked startled, her washed-out blue eyes opening wide. Those kind of interruptions were so unlike Becca who, of all the girls, understood the rhythm of a story.

"Shut up," Syl said and poked Becca with a sharp elbow.

Becca felt the wetness slip out, through her pants, soaking into the gold-coloured velour cushion. She started to cry, as much for the loss of the story as the damp spot she knew would soon be discovered.

"Look what baby did!" It was Shana who noticed first.

"Wet-pants, wet-pants!" cried Syl. "Gemma, she's disgusting."

"She's only a little girl, and you two are big ones."
Gemma picked Becca up and held her close, never minding the wetness now running down Becca's leg, not caring that Becca was squirming with embarrassment and rage and disappointment.

"I want the rest of the story," Becca cried. "I want the rest. I want the hall and the mist and the kiss and . . ."

"You know it already," said Gemma, and she carried Becca up the backstairs and ran a bath for her. Only when Becca was sitting in the bath, with the special bubbles mounding up on each side, did Gemma finish the story. Just for her. Syl and Shana refused to come in and listen.

CHAPTER

20

"We could have taken a train," Magda explained as they set out from the car rental. "It is much inex . . . how you say cheap. To change in Lublin."

"I checked," Becca said. "There are only two trains a day to Chelmno, and what would we do once we got there?" She steered the gray Fiat carefully onto Route 81, as Magda instructed her with a great flurry of hand-wavings. She was already thinking of the car as *Charger* as much for the expense on her Visa card as its reference to steeds of old.

"Walk," said Magda. "But I much appreciate the auto. The car."

"Besides," Becca continued, smiling, "I am a tourist. I want to see pretty places and take photographs and eat at good restaurants."

"Then I *very* much appreciate the car," Magda said. "Besides, if your grandmother had a palace, it would not do to walk. We must in the grand style. It would be . . . expected of the granddaughter. Of what? A countess? A princess?"

"Księżniczka," Becca said.

"You speak Polish!" Magda clapped her hands. "You

did not *tell* me." Then she made a grimace. "But what a *terrible* accent!"

"That was what my grandmother was called, before she came to America. We don't know if it was a title or a nickname."

"Pardon me, but what is a neekname?" Magda asked.

"A pet name, a family name," Becca explained.

"Ah, and I am called Kotek, which means little cat," Magda said. "By my mother and father first and sometimes still by my Auntie."

Becca was about to ask why when the route took a turn and a sign said PLOCK. Beside it, the land ran back flat and green, seemingly untouched.

"Isn't that one of our towns?" Becca asked.

"We are not interested," Magda said.

"Why not?"

"It is not of interest. There is a cathedral and then tall chimneys and they are . . ." her hands described a volcano.

"Spewing fire and smoke?" Becca asked.

"Yes, so. Exactly. One at the beginning of the city, one at the end, like on either side of books."

"Bookends," Becca said.

"So. We will stop in Torún. You will like it. It is famous for its . . . oh, I haven't the word. You will see when we are there."

"Can I guess?" Becca asked.

"It is a kind of cake, with wonderful spices. And baked in the shape of grand ladies and gentlemen. Maybe . . ." Magda looked impish, "even in the shape of a Księżniczka!" She pronounced it the way Becca had, and giggled.

"Gingerbread?" Becca guessed.

Magda shook her head, looking puzzled. "I am not sure."

The road to Torún was flat and they could see the Vistula, sometimes near, sometimes far, wide and grey, like clay.

"Roll down your window," Magda said, though the air

was crisp and cold. "Sometimes you can smell the cake baking in the factory."

But though they both drew in great breaths as they passed row after row of red brick buildings, Becca smelled nothing but a kind of old city odor until they stopped.

"Here," Magda said, "we will park and walk. It is best when you can to walk in a Polish city, yes?"

"Yes!" Becca agreed heartily.

They walked around admiring the older buildings, and stopped at last in a kind of cafe. They chose to sit outside under a nondescript umbrella that kept the intermittent sun from their faces.

Magda said, "I will order the cakes, but you must tell me if you are preferring coffee or tea."

"Tea, please," Becca said.

Within minutes they had a plateful of gingerbread nobility, with two cups of very dark tea in heavy white utilitarian ceramic mugs.

"Gingerbread," Becca pronounced.

"Gin-ger bread. Why not cake? Gin-ger cake?" Magda asked.

"I don't know," Becca admitted.

"We must discover this sometime," Magda said. "You are a journalist. You will find out and write to me the reason. You like gin-ger bread?"

"Yes and yes."

"Good," Magda said and, with a great grin, bit the head off of the gingery countess.

"You," Becca mumbled around her own bite of gingerbread, "are the most 'up' person I have ever met."

"Up. Yes. That is good?"

"Yes."

"What does it mean?" Magda's accent was, peculiarly, made less pronounced by her mouthful of cookie.

"It means optimistic. Happy. Full of joy."

"Ah, yes. But I am Polish."

"Is everybody who is Polish optimistic?"

"If one is not optimistic in Poland, then there is too

much to weep about," Magda said. "In the not-so-past history are many tragedies. Every family can recite them. The
blood of so many martyrs are still wet on our soil.
Once . . ." Her face took on a dreamy expression, the rest
of the gingerbread forgotten on her plate. "Once I was not
so optimistic. But I was young and did not know these
things and so can be forgiven. I was not so *up*. My mother
she was Jewish, my father Catholic. Only neither were . . .
were *doing* their religions."

"Practicing," Becca put in softly. "We would say practicing."

"How odd. To practice a religion, like a violin! What a
strange language English is." Magda giggled and her eyebrows danced left-right-left again. "I was not brought up
in either one."

Becca nodded and sipped her tea.

"Then one day our teacher saw that we knew little of
Poland's real history, not the history of heroes and gener-
als but the history of the people. Or rather that what we
knew of the immediate past we saw as the same kind of
thing—just history, but not real. Not having anything to do
with us. I am not saying this right."

"You are perfectly clear. Only drink your tea. It's getting cold."

Like an obedient little girl, Magda drank her tea down
in a single gulp. "Good. I like being perfectly clear. So our
teacher made us a trip. Do you have this in America?"

"Class trips? All the time. To places of Significant Historical Interest." Becca smiled. "To see history."

"She took us to Lublin. Outside of Lublin is Majdanek.
It was a camp during the war. There is a monument of
grey stones, a great mausoleum—that is the word?"

"Yes." Becca barely whispered.

"A mausoleum dedicated to the 360,000 men and
women and—she told us—even children of our own ages
who were murdered and discarded, like animal carcasses.
So close to where we lived. That is what she said. She told
us how the young like us, and the elderly like our grand-

parents, and the sick like Mr. Mleczko who cleaned our school but had bad lungs—were put into ovens. Burned up as if they had been meat. Or bread." She pushed the plate with the cake away from her with a sudden angry movement. "She said the children were whipped with cattle whips and their bodies piled onto lorries like filth, and taken to the *rose garden* which is what the guards called the gas-chamber. I remember every word she said.

"By then most of us were crying, some of the older boys were even sobbing loudly. And she said, 'See how green and lovely are the lawns around the memorial. Think of what horrors were buried here forty years ago right under our feet; think about what it is that has so fertilized this rich soil.' She made us look at the grey stones for a long time, then she had the bus take us home." Magda was silent for a moment. "She did not return to teach the next year."

"No," Becca said.

"No." Magda sighed. "I loved her very much. She was my first—oh love affair is the wrong word. I was eleven years old. She did not touch me in any way."

"We would say you had a crush on her."

"Crush?" Magda's hand described a downward arc, as if crushing something.

Becca nodded.

"How odd. Yet how true. My young heart was crushed, especially when she was not returned. She was a very good teacher."

"And . . ." Becca urged.

"Ah, you want an ending to the story. Not every story has an end, my friend, Becca."

"But, friend Magda, I suspect this one has."

Magda laughed delightedly and pulled the plate with the cake back towards her. She broke off a piece and put it in her mouth, rolling her eyes as if to emphasize how delicious it was. After she swallowed and dabbed at her lips in an exaggerated fashion with the cloth napkin, she sighed. "Oh, yes—an ending. From that day on I started practicing—yes?—being Jewish. I joined with other students who were Jewish and went to their homes for the holidays. Not all kept the holidays, you know. My mother did not approve."

"And your father?"

"He did not care. He just did not want me Catholic."

"Do you practice your Jewishness now?" Becca asked.

"I do not practice the holidays," Magda said.

"Celebrate."

"Yes—I do not practice or celebrate the holidays. I do not speak or read Hebrew. But I read history at University, and especially I read Holocaust history. I am member of the Polish Jewish Student League."

"That's how I got your name," Becca reminded her. "Through the Cracow group."

"Yes. So you see, if my teacher had not taken us to that horrible place, you and I would not become friends."

Becca smiled. "And I would not have had such splendid gingerbread."

They paid and left, walking arm-in-arm along the little boulevard. At first Becca was embarrassed, but after they passed many girls doing the same, she relaxed.

"And now to Chelmno?"

"I think we take a little longer and go west to Bydgoszcz. You will like the streets and buildings there. And soon it will be time for lunch."

"But we have just eaten," Becca said.

"Ah—but if you once smell *bigos* and pirogis, once you have a taste of *nalesniki*, you will not resist further."

"I have eaten all of those. Well, maybe not bigos. I live in a Polish farm community, you know."

Magda stopped, withdrew her arm from Becca's, and looked at her seriously. "But you have not yet eaten in *Poland*! First, though, I must show you the monument for Niklas Koppernigk. You would call him Nicolaus Copernicus. You have heard of him?"

"Of course I have heard of him."

"Well," Magda had gotten that twinkle in her eye again.

"I have heard how poorly Americans have their education. Nicolaus Copernicus was born here, in Torún. And there are many wonderful houses in the Old Town. I would love to live here some day, I think."

Becca smiled and decided that, for the rest of the day, she would play tourist and let Magda take her around. After that, she was determined to continue her search. Gemma, she was sure, would approve.

They ate lunch in a restaurant. Becca accepted what Magda ordered with good grace: a dish of strong stew, which was the bigos Magda had mentioned, and something that was a cross between a blintz and a crepe filled with cheese and covered with a sour cream sauce that was sweet and filling.

"If I ate like this every day," Becca warned, "I wouldn't even fit into the size twelve jeans I brought you." She paid for the entire meal, both hers and Magda's, and was surprised at how cheap it was.

They traveled on to Bydgoszcz, past fields of yellow lupine blowing distractedly in the intermittent breezes. Overhead the white clouds looked fresh-washed. Willows stood knee-deep in pockets of the river, not the weeping kind that Becca was used to, but a variety that lifted its branches straight up from massive trunks. Becca commented on them.

"They do not grow that way by nature," Magda explained, "but we cut them back to get branches to make baskets. You know baskets?"

"Willow baskets!" Becca exclaimed. "I never thought they were made of *willow*!"

"You Americans never stop to be an amazement!" Magda said.

"Cease to amaze me," corrected Becca.

"Yes."

Becca pulled along the shoulder of the road and stopped the car.

"A photograph?" asked Magda.

"Yes—you and the willows."

"Only I do not stand in the water. I do not grow well that way!" Magda giggled at her joke and Becca joined her laughter. She took the picture while they were both still laughing, then took a second just in case.

Once more on the road they passed large fields and then stands of white birch, gleaming in the afternoon light.

"I love birch trees," Becca commented. "We have one with a triple trunk on our front lawn."

"The birch is a favorite to me, too," Magda said. "Do you know what the birch tree means in Poland?"

"No." Becca glanced over at her.

"My professor told me. Once it was believed birch trees housed souls of the dead. Even today, at Pentecost, what we call Zielone Świątki, the Green Holiday, people cut down branches of the birch and bring it into the house to put around the windows. It is a bit pagan here still, yes?"

Becca looked back at the road. "Must have been a lot of birch trees at Majdanek."

Magda made a strange sound, something between a cough and a sigh. "My friend, Becca, there are birch trees everywhere in Poland."

They arrived an hour later in Bydgoszcz and booked into a hotel, the Brda.

"First time I ever stayed in a hotel without vowels," Becca commented as they unpacked.

Magda shook her head. "There are two towels in the bath, Becca. This is not so poor a country as that. The hotel has three stars."

Becca tried a few times to explain the joke, realized there *was* a vowel after all, and gave it up as a bad joke. They went downstairs for a walk. The evening, though, had begun to turn chilly. Becca was glad for the sweater she had brought along, but Magda was still in a short-sleeved blouse. When Becca saw her shiver surreptitiously, she announced: "I am cold, Magda, even through my sweater. Let's go back to the hotel."

Magda gave her no argument. But as they walked, they planned the trip for the next day.

"It is only one half hour if you drive, Becca," Magda said.

"How long if *you* drive?"

"Forever, I am afraid. I do not drive in auto . . . in cars," Magda said. "I cannot afford a car and I live in Warsaw. We have trains and buses to every place I want to go. But is it true everyone in America has at least one car?"

"Not quite *everyone*," Becca said.

"Do you?"

"Of course. But I live in the country," Becca said quickly. "And there are no buses or trains that come near my house."

"No buses, no trains." Clearly it was a stunning idea to Magda.

They reached the hotel still deep in a discussion of transportation, and went right into the hotel's dining room. Though Becca swore she couldn't eat a thing, still being full from lunch, the waiter—who spoke English, even better than Magda—with Magda's help ordered her a full meal. When it came, the medallions of veal and the thin, delicate French fries were too appealing to resist. Becca finished them, the small green peas, and a piece of cream cake besides.

"Tomorrow you will try borscht," Magda said.

"My grandmother made borscht," Becca said. "No thank you. Hot beet soup . . . !" She wrinkled her nose.

"You have never had it in Poland," Magda said.

They slept in the narrow twin beds. Auntie was wrong. Magda sometimes snored, though lightly. Becca suspected it was because of the unfamiliar mattress. By the time she finally fell asleep, those light snores were the only sound in the hotel.

CHAPTER

21

"The prince walked along the path of the overgrown forest, the thorns opening before him. On either side of the path white birch trees gleamed like the souls of the new dead."

"I wish you wouldn't say that part, Gemma," Sylvia whispered. *"Not on Halloween."*

"It is as true on Halloween as any other time," Gemma said.

"It's not true ever!*"* said Shana.

"Is," Becca said. *"Is, too."* She was dressed like a princess, with a crown and scepter even though Shana had insisted only kings carried those.

"Is not!" Shana was a pirate. Her wicked black shoe-polish moustache shone with perspiration. She was wearing long underwear for the walk between houses.

"Is, too." Becca turned to Gemma for support. Gemma simply continued the story.

"Then at last he came to the palace itself. A mist still lay all about the walls and floors, hovering like a last breath on the lips of all the sleepers." She stopped to take a breath.

"Not on Halloween, Gemma," Sylvia said, getting up,

*the handmade tutu of her ballerina costume sticking up at
an odd angle and making her exit somewhat less dramatic
than she had hoped.*

Shana followed Sylvia out of the room, pirate sword
dragging. The year before, the sword had belonged to Sylvia's king costume and Shana had coveted it for 364 days.
Now she was annoyed that it banged into her heels when
she walked. It was that, and the hot underwear, rather than
the story, that were making her cranky. But Becca was only
eight years old. There was no way she could understand.

"Go on, Gemma, go on," Becca said.

Gemma went on, needing little encouragement where
Sleeping Beauty was concerned.

CHAPTER

22

Magda rose early and left the room. Becca heard her go and turned over, falling back to sleep at once, jet lag having overcome her desire to start on the day. By the time she woke again, sunlight was streaming into the room and Magda was sitting reading in the one chair.

"I overslept," Becca said apologetically.

"You missed breakfast," Magda said, her mouth for once unsmiling.

"That's all right."

Magda grinned and pointed to the dresser. "I brought up a bun."

Becca sat up in bed. "I really don't need anything."

"You will need your strength. We go now to Chelmno and I have been reading about it. Do you want to hear?"

"I already read quite enough about it before coming. It was . . ." Becca hesitated. "It was not a pleasant place."

"It was worse than Majdanek. There, at least, was some hope for the strong."

Becca grimaced. "I already know."

"Then why . . ." Magda came over to sit on her own bed and stare at Becca. "Then why are you here?"

"Because this is where my grandmother's trail seems to begin. I don't know why."

"Perhaps she lived in one of the nearby towns, or in the Lodz ghetto. The Jewish ghetto," Magda said. "It is written here in the pamphlet that the Nazis rounded up—that is the word?—yes, rounded up thousands from Lodz and the little Jewish towns and brought them by cart and by railroad to Chelmno. Maybe your grandmother's family died that way but she was somehow hidden, undiscovered. It could have happened."

"Yes, it could have. No woman escaped from Chelmno," Becca said. "At least that is what I was told." She shivered.

"We do not have to go there. We can go instead to the Biaiowieza Forest. It is not far. The Polish kings used to go to the hunt there. It still has bison. You know bison? And . . ." She stopped because Becca stood up abruptly. "You are not interested in forests and bison."

Becca turned. "No."

"You are not interested in the hunting places of kings."

"I am sorry, but no."

"I am not either. But . . ." Magda shrugged. "Sometimes it is important for a friend to ask these things."

Becca nodded. "I'll be ready shortly."

They headed northeast along route 83 and several small towns later came into the city of Swiecle. There they turned south, crossing over the winding Narew River, broad and slow-moving. A little further along the flat, unvarying route, they came to a small sign: CHELMNO. Ahead was a white church spire.

The grey day at that very moment decided to shake off its dull coat. The sun shone through the fragments of clouds with such sudden ferocity that as they came into the village, Becca was temporarily blinded. When she could see again, they were almost upon a large wooden wagon with high plank back and sides. She braked quickly, throwing them both forward against the seat belts.

"Ouf!" Magda said, and followed it with something sharp in Polish.

"Horse-drawn wagons," commented Becca. "It's another century here."

Magda giggled and smoothed down her hair. "I have seen this in an American movie. Going back to the past."

The drive through the town—once they got around the wagon—took less than five minutes. Chelmno was a mud-colored place except for the church, which gleamed white and solid and very out of place in the dun village. The houses lining the street were low; some looked rotted through. Then the greyness of the day was reasserted by the overhead clouds, and it was as if the air became the same color as the buildings.

Becca turned at the far end of the village and headed back, pulling up next to the church. Shutting off the engine, she asked Magda: "What do you think?"

"It is a very odd place."

"Odd for a Polish village?"

"No. It is very Polish. But odd because to read the pamphlet, it was a place of such horror. Where would you put 300,000 people, even dead?"

Becca shuddered at her matter-of-fact tone.

"And it is so ordinary. So quiet. So undistinguished."

Opening her door, Becca stepped out. She took a deep breath as if that might bring her some scent of an evil that was fifty years disguised. All she smelt was the horse pulling the cart as it came up even with the car and went past. Magda got out and stood next to her silently.

An old woman in a drab, proletarian coat reaching her knees walked by across the street.

"Ask her," Becca urged Magda. "Ask her."

"Ask her what?"

"Ask her—where was the concentration camp. What happened here? Is there anyone around who was here then? Would she look at my grandmother's photos? Anything."

Magda nodded and ran across the muddy road. When

she reached the old woman, she began to speak quickly, gesturing eagerly with her hands. The old woman turned her head once to look at Magda, then turned and walked away, head down. After a few more steps, Magda quit following her and crossed back over.

"Well?"

"You saw. She would not speak with me."

They looked up and down the road. "There!" Becca said. "There are some men. Let's ask them." She pulled Magda along.

The small knot of men they approached were in dark clothes and stared at the strangers with sullen eyes. There were five of them, three smoking cigarettes with such ferocity Becca was sure their moustaches were in danger of going up in flames. Magda began to speak even before they were close. One man growled something that sounded like "Braaaagh," and turned away sharply, his hand suggesting they leave. A second suddenly found great interest in his own pockets, searching for what eventually turned out to be a cigarette and matches. The third and fourth merely glared at them, but the fifth, a man no more than fifty, wearing a dark cloth cap, spoke volumes with his hands as he talked in rapid Polish. Becca was glad she didn't understand the words.

Magda held her own hands up as if to contain the waterfall of words. Finally, without replying, she grabbed Becca and turned her around, shepherding them both back to the car, away from the man whose voice seemed to rise in direct proportion to their escape.

"What did he say?" Becca asked when they were close to the sanctuary of the Fiat.

"He said nothing worth the repeat."

"He said a lot."

"It was filth. Better not to know."

"I must." Becca put her hands on Magda's shoulder and looked directly into her eyes. "I must."

"He said that nothing happened here and that we should

take our Jew questions away or that the nothing would happen again." Magda's shoulders were shaking.

"*Prezepraszam.*" It was the old woman who had refused Magda's questions earlier. "*Prezepraszam.*"

Magda turned to her and the old woman spoke quickly, pointing towards the church where, as it happened, a round-faced priest in a black cassock was emerging. Then ducking her head, as if warding off a blow, the old woman scurried, beetlelike, down the street.

"What did she say?" Becca asked. "Why did she point to the church?"

"She said that the only one who could tell us anything is the priest. He is the only one who will talk to us about these things. She said not to ask the people anything. Especially not the men. But the priest, she said, is the one to ask."

"Enter the priest," Becca said. "Right on cue. Do you think he knows anything? He doesn't look old enough to have been here fifty years ago."

"Priests in these little villages know all the secrets," Magda said. "After all, they hear confession."

"But I thought," Becca whispered, "I thought confessions were secret."

"*Secret* does not include history," Magda said. She walked up the church path and intercepted the priest, speaking quickly and quietly.

"It is okay," the priest said, loud enough for Becca to hear. "I was a year in America. In Boston College. I am speaking English. Please to call me Father Stashu."

"I am Rebecca Berlin and this is my friend—and my translator—Magda Bronski," Becca called back.

"Pardon me if I ask, but Chelmno is not a usual stop for tourists. Not even tourists—" and he looked piercingly at Becca—"on the Holocaust tours."

Irritated, Becca asked, more pointedly than she meant to, "Do I look Jewish?"

Father Stashu smiled. "Not at all. But Americans who find their way to this part of Poland are almost always looking for the monuments. There are no monuments here in Chelmno. And the people do not like to talk about what happened."

"Father Stashu," Magda said, "I do not wish to be insulting to your intelligence or ours, but 300,000 people died here. How can you not want to talk of it?"

The priest's pink cheeks turned even pinker, as if burnished by her remarks. "I did not say, my child, that *I* would not talk of it. I have made a great study of the evil that happened here. But the people who lived through it do not like to discuss it. Especially not to strangers. It is making them uncomfortable."

"Uncomfortable!" Becca exclaimed.

"When I first came here twenty years ago, I thought to make a place . . . a career in the church. A few years in little place like this, move on to larger city, and maybe become bishop. You know, a Polish priest can aspire to greatness in these times." He chuckled, but when they did not join in his little joke, he quickly went on. "But when I began to learn what happened here fifty years ago—well, it was only thirty years ago then—I knew I had to stay to help these poor people cleanse their souls. It became my life's work."

"How can you cleanse them . . ." Magda began.

". . . if they will not talk about it?" Becca finished for her.

"Come, my daughters, walk a bit with me, and I will explain it to you." He led them, an arm through each of theirs, across the street, stepping over a small ditch filled with muddy water. "This, you see, was where the Nazi schoolteacher and his wife lived. There were Nazis imported here, homesteading, you see. They brought in good party members to colonize—to make German—this town. They gave it a new name."

"Kulmhof," Becca whispered.

"Ah, yes—you have done your homework. There are no Germans left here now. Only Poles. But that does not excuse them, my poor people. If you ask them, they will tell you they were as much victims as were the Jews. But they do not in their very hearts believe that. Only sometimes in the confessional will they cry to me. Only sometimes, on their deathbeds, will they tell me they fear dying because they will have to confront the souls of all those murdered Jews. And Gypsies. And other Poles, too—Communists and protesters. And a few priests, as well."

They were walking along the road now, away from the church, and Father Stashu guided them past a dirty barricade, past some broken-down stone outbuildings, the whole thing the color of the muddy road.

"And I say to them that if they are truly repentant, God will forgive them. And if God forgives them, they will also be forgiven by the souls of the Jews and Gypsies and Communists and priests." He smiled, but the corners of his mouth turned down instead of up and his eyes did not look as if they were smiling.

"You do not sound—forgive me for saying this, Father—terribly convinced," Magda said.

Becca bit her lower lip. It was just what she had been thinking.

"When I was twenty-three and coming here for the first time, I was convinced of the truth of what I have just told you. But I have been here now twenty years, and each year I learn more about what happened then. It is hard to keep one's faith with that knowledge. But I try." He stopped and released their arms. "This, *schloss*, for example."

"*Schloss! Schloss!* This is a *schloss*!" Magda's voice had risen.

"Magda, what is it?" Becca asked, a sudden chill descending upon her. The sun was completely behind the clouds now and an ominous rumbling came from the north, thunder of course, but somehow also like the sound of trucks over cobbles.

"A *schloss* is a castle, Becca. A *castle*."

Becca turned around quickly. The ruined buildings looked more like farm stockbarns than anything else. The cobbled stones in the road were uneven, many of them missing. "Castle?"

"It was an old castle once. Ruined in World War I," the priest explained. "But it was here that the prisoners were brought. The Nazis said it was for baths, for delousing. But it was only for death."

Becca reached out a hand and Magda took it, steadying her. "A castle," she said.

"Not much of one, really," Father Stashu was saying. "Not even before World War I."

But Becca did not hear him. She was trying her best to catch her breath, to stop shaking. With Magda's arms around her, she breathed deeply several times. Father Stashu looked at her in alarm. "My child . . ."

Magda looked up. "She is all right, Father. Perhaps we should go back now to the car."

"Come to the church. I will make us coffee. I have some little cakes. You will be fine. Now you see why I could not leave. There is much here that needs to be atoned for. You feel it, too."

Downstairs in the church, in the priest's study, they sat and had tea cakes and some of his very strong coffee in the same kind of white ceramic mugs they had drunk from in the Torún cafe. Father Stashu spoke about spring and summer in the Lublin Upland, where he had been born, with its long, narrow fields, gentle slopes of hills, winding ravines, old untouched forests.

"I rarely get there now," he said. "But when I do, it renews my soul."

"This coffee and these cakes have renewed mine," Becca said. "Thanks." She was no longer shaking.

"Did you have family who died at Chelmno, then?" Father Stashu asked. He took the empty cups from them and put them on a little serving table. "Or are you more than a little psychical. Is that the word?"

"I don't know," Becca said. "I came here to find that out. About my family."

Father Stashu sat back in his chair. He folded his hands, lacing his fingers artlessly under his chin. The pink spots on his cheeks were pale in the greying light of the room. "Where are you staying?"

"In Bydgoszcz, at the Brda Hotel," Magda said.

"That is good. I have a friend who is in Bydgoszcz— Josef Potocki. He was a partisan in the war. He lives there now, though he could live anywhere in the world. Like me, he is drawn back by the souls of the dead. If I know much about what happens now in Chelmno, he knows everything about what happened then. But unlike my poor flock, he will tell you anything he feels you need to know. Let me call him."

Becca and Magda exchanged quick glances.

"Tell him we will be at the hotel this evening. After dinner. We will have coffee."

Father Stashu smiled, stood, and went to the wall where there was an old-fashioned telephone. He dialed the number, turning as he did so to Becca. "He is not always at home, but ... ah, good ... Josef!" The torrent of Polish that followed was incomprehensible to Becca, but Magda followed it closely, nodding in agreement at the things the priest was saying.

Before the conversation came to a close, with several obvious effusions, Magda had whispered, "Good. He can be there."

"Josef will be happy to see you this evening, my children," Father Stashu said after hanging up the phone. "But he is an old man, and rather frail, so do not tire him too much."

"We won't," Becca promised.

"And if you go out the way I show you, you will come to a beautiful part of the Narew River. Even on such a grey day, it will have its own brightness. And its own peace. That peace ... it is almost a miracle, considering ..." For a moment he was silent. Then he looked at the ceiling. "I cannot forgive them, you know. I can love them but I cannot forgive them. But then—I do not have to. I am not God."

They followed his instructions and came to a place where the river was gentle, glassy, and winding past patches of trees, the dark trunks thrusting out from the banks. On the other side of the river were more fields, and the town church spired up past a barrier of trees. To their right was a great field, surrounded on three sides by trees, on the fourth by the river. Odd stone walls marked out long rectangular building sites. There were no buildings.

"Listen," Becca said.

Magda listened. "What is it? I hear nothing."

"Exactly," Becca said. "Isn't that odd?"

The two of them listened for a while to the silence. Then, without speaking, they got back into the car and drove away.

CHAPTER

23

"As he walked through the castle, he marveled at how many lay asleep: the good people, the not-so-good, the young people and the not-so-young, and not one of them stirring. Not one."

"What is stirring, Gemma?" Becca asked as they walked through the Three Country Fair. She felt very grown up because it was her first time going to the Fair in the evening. There was so much to see, she had scarcely paid attention to the beginning of the story. But as she and Gemma waited for their turn on the Ferris wheel—Shana and Syl already on their second loop around—Gemma had started Briar Rose to keep Becca from becoming overexcited.

But that word . . . *"What is stirring, Gemma? Like stirring the soup? With a spoon? Why would they have soup spoons when they were sleeping? Why would they want to be making soup when they're lying down? I don't get it. I don't . . ."* Her voice, in her excitement, had kept rising.

"Stirring means moving about, waking up," Gemma said, holding tight to her hand.

"Then why not say that? Why not say, 'and not one of them moving about. Not one of them getting up'? Why say

stirring. That's like soup, Gemma. That's silly. And Sleep-ing Beauty isn't a silly story."

"No," Gemma said, her voice suddenly quiet, thought-ful; her eyes far away though she was staring at the Ferris wheel. "Not a silly story at all."

"Then why say stir, Gemma?" Becca asked again.

Gemma didn't answer this time, but simply pulled her along into the waiting chair where fear and anticipation so mingled with the whoosh *of the rocking seat being lifted, that the story was forgotten as Becca cried out: "Oh, Gemma, oh Gemma—look at the sky!"*

CHAPTER

24

They sat in the lounge, fresh coffee in their cups, and waited without speaking for Josef Potocki.

Becca thought about the ride back from Chelmno, with the day darkening around them: first a grey mist off the Narew, then the clouds closing entirely over the sky, and at last a steady drizzle which accompanied them the rest of the way. Neither had wanted to explore the city in that rain and they had rested in their room, reading books. Becca's book was a history of Poland and she had been surprised to find the name *Potocki* as one of the aristocratic families known in southern Poland since the thirteenth century.

"Do you think our Josef Potocki is of royal blood?" she asked, her voice a sudden intrusion into the silence of their room.

"We have no royalty in Poland anymore," Magda said shortly. Then she laughed. "Anyone can shorten his name or change it. You see princes and castles everywhere."

"That *schloss* . . ." Becca began.

"If *that* was your grandmother's castle, she was from a very poor family indeed," Magda said.

They were both silent for a long moment, then Becca

said suddenly, "You think I am foolish about this quest? My sisters think it's crazy."

"It is not crazy to want to know the past. It is only crazy to live there, like so many of the aristocracy." Magda smiled. "Come, it is dinner time."

Dinner had hardly interested either of them and they had picked at their food. The coffee and cake were the only things Becca had eaten with any gusto. The wait in the lounge, fresh coffee in their cups, seemed endless.

"What time is it?" Becca asked, not for the first time.

"He said eight o'clock. It is but half eight," Magda answered. "The past has been waiting for fifty years or more, Becca. Another hour more or less . . ." She laughed. "I sound like Auntie to you and you are older than I."

Becca returned the laugh. "You're right. I'm being a goose."

"Goose? How is this a goose?"

"Goose, ninny, el stupido, nitwit . . ."

"Ah, I know nitwit. I had a boyfriend who was American. He would slap his hand to his head so . . ." She demonstrated. " '*Such* a nitwit,' he would say. So a nitwit is a goose. A nine-y?"

"Ninny."

"Good, I learn more English. And El stu . . ."

"El Stupido. Not English exactly. Spanish. Well, not really."

"I will keep *goose*, I think," Magda said. She slapped her hand to her head. "*Such* a goose!"

They both laughed uproariously.

"It is good to hear such laughter on a night like this." The voice was smooth, cultured, with British intonations, a bit high-pitched with age. "Are you the two young women looking for Josef Potocki?" There was a self-mocking undertone to it. A tall, thin man stepped into the little bit of light thrown by the table lamp. He had prominent high cheekbones that gave an oriental cast to his eyes, and a perfectly straight nose. His mouth was large and mobile and firmer than his age demanded. He leaned

on a silver-headed walking stick. The hand holding the
stick was livered with spots, the only real indication of his
years, but the grip seemed very firm.

"Yes," they spoke together, and Magda was quick to in-
troduce them.

He sat down in the one chair left and, with an easy
wave of a hand, signaled to the waiter. Coffee was brought
to him at once and it was clear he was a well-known fig-
ure at the Brda.

"So you wish to know about Chelmno?" he asked. The
way he said the word, it was almost a curse, but one spoken so often that the very familiarity had leached out its
power to damn.

"Yes," Becca said. She leaned forward. "At least I think
I do. You see, my grandmother may have come from
there."

"Was she Jewish?" Potocki asked. "I do not ask this
with any imputation. I merely ask, you see."

"Yes," Becca said. "She was."

"Then she could not have come from that place." He
said it simply.

"May I tell you what I know?" asked Becca.

"Please proceed." He took a sip of the coffee, put it
down, then sat back in the chair, the wings of which nearly
obscured his face.

Becca spoke quickly about Gemma, about her death,
about the papers with the name of Gitl Mandlestein, about
the single word Kulmhof that had led her all the way to
Poland. "And I have photographs of her as she was in the
refugee camp in Fort Oswego. And other things."

"May I see the pictures?" Potocki's voice was now
somewhat brittle and suddenly tired. Becca realized that he
must have replayed this same sort of scene many times
with many travelers searching for loved ones. His hand
reached out. It shook a bit with age.

Becca slipped one of the photographs from the folder
and handed it across to him. "The child is my mother. The

photo is dated 1945, as you can see. That is really all I know."

He took the picture and settled back against the chair, and though she could see the hand with the photo, she couldn't see his face. She waited for some reaction, but when it came, it was not at all what she'd expected. There was a soft odd sound, a *shu-shu-shu*. After a second Becca realized that he was sobbing quietly.

Leaping from her chair, Magda bent over him, speaking rapidly in Polish, then calling for the waiter to bring something—a glass of water, perhaps, or a towel.

Potoki took a linen handkerchief from his pocket and leaned forward. The handkerchief had entwined initials in dark blue. He dabbed at his eyes. "The dead," he said. "The dead come back to life so unexpectedly." He looked over at Becca, as if studying her face. "Of course—I should have seen it at once. You are her. Księżniczka."

Becca felt her hands begin to tremble. Suddenly she saw it all. The initials on the handkerchief were JMP, just like the ring. She took the passport picture of the man from the folder and stared at it. How could *she* have not seen. It was Potocki, very young and very handsome. She wondered that none of them—her mother and sisters and she— looked at all like him. Taking a deep breath and willing her hands to be still, she said at last, "So, you are . . . you are my grandfather." She was stunned by the simplicity of it all. She took the ring from her pocketbook and held it out to him.

He began to chuckle then, and then to laugh, not a great belly of a laugh but a very sedate and frail laugh. Putting the handkerchief up to his mouth and then to his eyes again, he shook his head. "No, no, no, child, this is not possible." He spoke to Magda quickly in Polish and Magda, too, laughed and sat back down in her own chair.

"He says, Becca, that the ring is his, but . . ." The laugh returned for a moment. "But he cannot possibly be your grandfather. He is . . . he has always been . . . I do not know how to say this in English." She turned to Potocki and shrugged.

"I do not make love to women," he said simply, "though I have loved many as friends."

"You're gay?" Becca said with sharp surprise.

"The American expression is so . . ." he shrugged with a wry smile. "In my life *gaiety* has not been the dominant factor. But I am certainly—in your word—gay. It was why the Nazis interned me. Even with my family connections. I cannot possibly be your grandfather. But I knew your grandmother."

"And my grandfather?"

"*And* your . . . grandfather. They were with me."

Becca drew a deep breath. "In Chelmno? In the camp?"

"In the woods. We were partisans. It is a long story. Too long for tonight. This shock has tired me. Come to my house tomorrow and I will tell it to you."

He rose and Becca could see that both his hands were trembling.

"Forgive me my lack of strength. I look forward to to-morrow." He bowed slightly and reached into the breast pocket of his jacket. Taking out a silver card case, he held it to her. "Open this, my dear. My hands are too stiff. The card has my address. I will expect you at eleven. For lunch of course." He bowed to Magda as well. "Both of you are expected. You are, I am sure, not like most young people and will be on time."

Becca took the card, and he returned the case to his pocket. Then, bent over his stick, he walked away from them and the doors seemed to open magically before him. Becca knew there were doormen and waiters doing the ac-tual mechanics, but she liked the thought that—like the thornbush in Gemma's story—the doors were parting be-cause he was some kind of prince.

"Well!" Magda said when he was gone, "there *is* an ending to your fairy tale."

"Or at least a middle," Becca said. Then, she added, "I hope he doesn't die in the night."

"I think," Magda said, suddenly quite serious, "that there is a man who will not let death take him by the hand until he has finished what he has begun."

"I think you are right," Becca answered as solemnly.

Josef Potoki's house was made of brick and stone and had been built in the middle of the last century. When they rang the bell, the door was opened by a plump, pleasant-looking woman dressed in a conservative dark dress with white piping around the collar. She spoke only Polish, so Magda explained.

"He is waiting for us in the drawing room. *Drawing* room? This is right?"

The room was a combination of living room and library. There was a fireplace with a fire spitting sparks and just settling down. Three stuffed chairs in a semicircle around a table by the hearth sat like a welcoming family. Potoki was already in command of the one closest to the fire.

"Come in, come in, my young friends. The story is a long one, so you must make yourselves comfortable. We will have a light lunch, and tea around four, and dinner—if the story is still ongoing—in here. In the dining room if I have finished by then. Do not worry. It is not dull. It will not be a bore. Some of it will be about your grandmother. Not all. She is only a part of a very large tale, as you will see. But I will try and stick as close to her part as I can. Księżniczka. Księżniczka. You are so like her indeed. Tell me, did she have a good life, child?"

Becca sat down on his right, in a chair with a floral pattern of red and gold. "I think so. She had the one daughter and three granddaughters. She worked hard. I . . . we . . . all loved her very, very much. We lived together, all in the one house."

"A large house?"

"A very large house, sir."

"Ah . . . she would have liked that. And did she never marry again?"

"Again?"

He smiled. "She told you nothing then."

"All she ever told us was the story of Briar Rose."

Potocki looked inquiringly at Magda, who reeled off a quick Polish sentence. Then he turned and smiled again. "The fairy tale *La Belle au Bois Dormant*." His French was flawless. "I understand."

"I don't," Becca said.

"You will. You will." And without further introduction, he began the promised story, telling it with a practiced economy, as if he were only a storyteller and not one of the main characters.

CASTLE

The thirteenth fairy,
her fingers as long and thin as straws,
her eyes burnt by cigarettes,
her uterus an empty teacup,
arrived with an evil gift.

> —Anne Sexton,
> *from "Briar Rose (Sleeping Beauty)"*
> Transformations

Once we have accepted the story we cannot escape the
story's fate.

> —P.L. Travers: About the Sleeping Beauty

CHAPTER

25

You must understand (he said) that this is a story of survivors, not heroes. The war was full of them. A man is not a hero if he scrabbles to stay alive, if he struggles for one more crust of bread, one more ragged breath. We were all heroes of the moment. None more than Josef P.

He was born the last child and late of a large family whose connection with the aristocracy was more a matter of long memory than money. When his father died, his still beautiful mother remarried almost at once, causing the more knowledgeable to put truth to the rumors of her affair with the local Potocki heir. Josef was sent away, much too young, to a British public school where his looks—ugly for a child, but quite beautiful for an adolescent raised at a time when stories of faery abandonment were current in certain circles—brought him both abuse and favoritism. He was first bullied unmercifully, a British specialty, and then doted upon by both the masters and the top boys. He managed by sheer stupidity, really, to keep his virtue until he entered the university where a particularly persistent tutor managed to instruct him in both Dante and the acts of love. He believed at that point that he would never go home to Poland again and adopted his stepfather's last name and title because in England he had become a snob.

He was wrong in many things, but never about his feelings. And he found he had three aptitudes: for the theater, for political amnesia, and for love.

He took a first at college, more by accident than study, and went immediately to Paris where he discovered a fourth aptitude—for the demimonde life. To say he survived it is to point out the obvious. To say he *understood* his survival is to credit him with more introspection than he—at the moment—actually had. He went from Paris to Vienna to Berlin with as little thought, writing for the small theaters and being passionate about his leading men.

He was on the cusp of his thirtieth birthday, determined to enjoy every last minute of it, in Berlin in 1936. He was in love with the most perfectly Aryan-looking boy of twenty-two. The boy had a shock of white blond hair, even teeth, a Greek nose, and cornflower blue eyes. His name was Adam Gottlieb. He was a Jew. But under Potocki's protection—Prince Potocki as he was known in the theater circles—Adam was safe. They changed his name to Alan Berg, Alan of the Mountains, and everyone conveniently forgot that he was Jewish. Especially Josef P.

Josef loved it best when he and his Alan drove out into the mountains on holidays, staying in the small chalets, and hiking for days. He used to crown Alan with twinings of edelweiss and they would gaze out over the high peaks, singing songs from the latest cabaret shows. It was as close as Josef would ever get to heaven.

They were, of course, living in the belly of the wolf. They never thought *they* would be devoured. Apolitical, noticing only each other, quoting Goethe and Schiller and the darkly sensual verses of Rimbaud and Baudelaire ("May they come, may they come," Alan would sing over and over, "the days which enchant us.") they were surprised when the world overtook them. Their first real shock came when they entered the town where they had rented a new chalet. A banner was suspended over the road: JEWS ENTER AT THEIR OWN RISK.

For a moment Josef could not understand why Alan had cried out. Then he reached over and touched Alan softly on the shoulder, careful not to disturb his driving, but nevertheless to assure him Josef thought the banner a hateful thing.

"No one will know," Josef whispered.

"I know," Alan said. "It is enough." His shoulder shuddered beneath Josef's hand.

"In Bavaria . . ." Josef said, meaning he had hoped that in such a small village politics would play no part. But when they pulled up in front of the hotel that rented out the chalets, there was a sign on the door: "Dogs and Jews not allowed."

"I will not stay," Alan said. "I will not." His arms shook with the tension of holding his hands still on the wheel.

"They will not know," Josef said again, not understanding it was the wrong thing to say, not realizing the gulf that had suddenly opened between them. "How could they know?"

Alan did not even try to respond and so, foolishly Josef said the final thing to divide them and did not till years later understand what he had done. "But we have been looking forward to going away together, and it is just a stupid sign. What harm can it do us? Look—we will not even eat in the dining room. I will cook for us in the chalet. I will even go in now and get the keys. You do not have to do any of that."

Alan shuddered but said nothing more.

They stayed only overnight, sleeping in separate beds. The next morning they returned to Berlin, fighting bitterly all the way, but never mentioning politics. Josef did not see him again. Alan fled first to Paris, then later—Josef heard—to Palestine where he died in some silly border squabble. Such a waste of a beautiful life, Josef thought then, raging mindlessly at the desertion. But years later, sitting in a dark forest, outside of Kulmhof, he realized

Jane Yolen

that Alan had gone down fighting and that was, in itself, a good thing. He had even quoted Charles Darney's final speech in Alan's memory, with as much theatricality as a quarter bottle of cognac could lend him.

"I believe it was God's will to send a boy forth from this land to the Reich, to let him grow to manhood, to raise him to be Führer of the nation. . . ."

He listened to that speech over the radio in the arms of his Viennese lover. It was 1938 and Josef believed his lover who was, after all, high up in von Schuschnigg's government, when he said that Hitler was a false, wretched liar who did not stand a chance against the strength of the Austrian people.

"We are a people," he had told Josef, "who have more culture in our noses than this paperhanger has in his behind."

It was the crudest thing Josef had ever heard his lover say and Josef giggled nervously at it. He refused to hear the false bravado, the utter fear behind the boast. How could he? They rarely talked politics. They rarely talked at all. They ate together, long leisurely meals. They slept together. It was enough.

They made love during Hitler's victory speech, a horrible, angry, passionate thrusting, that left Josef bruised and somewhat stunned. He had planned to have a long talk with his lover about being more gentle the next morning. But when he woke, he found the man dead in the marble bath, his wrists still bleeding soft red lines into the tub. There was no note, but the blood was like scripting in the water, and even Josef could read that. He fled, carrying only an overnight case, crossing back into Germany, though by then the borders between Germany and Austria were only paper formalities.

Why did he stay in Germany? Why did anyone stay? The music still played in the cafes and nightclubs: "At Katrina's with the golden hair . . . tum-de-dum . . . The boys and girls are dancing there . . . tum-de-dum . . ." The drinks were cheap. The theaters were still open. And Josef was not Jewish. He turned his eyes away from the yellow stars on the coats, the beatings. Hadn't he survived his own floggings in school, survived his own tauntings? And the music still played in the cafes.

Why did he stay in Germany? Why did anyone stay? There was an electric current of national pride in the air. Wine ran like blood from the open necks of bottles in the beer halls. Slogans charged the walls of every street. And there was the humor—*Galgenhumor*, gallows humor— which they all shared and which made everyone laugh. So much laughter. Jokes like: Have you seen the German Forest brand suits that began to swell in the spring and change color in the fall? He did not really notice when the Communists began to disappear, and the Gypsies. He had a protector in the Berlin government. They laughed at the Führer, that ugly little man, but only at night, only in bed, only within the circle of their own arms. And the music still played in the cafes.

Why did he stay in Germany? Why did anyone stay? Children on the street corners jumped rope to rhymes:

> *Handschen falten, kopfchen senken,*
> *Und an Adolf Hitler denken.*

> *Fold your little hands, lower your little head,*
> *And think of Adolf Hitler.*

The pamphlets about the Jews multiplied. He heard rumors of internment camps for antisocial elements like Jehovah's Witnesses and socialists. And faggots. The kind who cross-dressed and were flagrant in their habits. The kind who sang falsetto and approached men in the streets. The kind who frequented the homosexual bars. The kind who had to wear pink triangles. The 175ers. He did not have a lover for a year. But the music still played in the cafes.

* * *

The persecution—systematic and horrible—against the homosexuals had begun as early as 1933. Some part of Josef must have known. But it was mostly rumor. He was good at dismissing rumor. And the men who disappeared weren't *just* homosexuals. They were also known agitators—politically outspoken or garishly arrayed. Not doctors. Not Lawyers. Not playwrights. With his dark, masculine good looks, with his family connections, with his protectors who were also protecting themselves, Josef never thought the pink triangle laws were meant for him.

But he stopped going to the theaters and bars and cafes. He stopped frequenting parties where men were the only guests. He hid even from himself, dating women of limited virtue. He even made limited love to one of them. Only one.

In the end, of course, he was found out. After the 1934 Roehm Putsch it was inevitable. It is only remarkable that he was not found out until the end of 1940.

His arrest happened in such a banal manner, he almost hated telling of it. He was reported on by his landlady who had discovered—so she said—literature of an unnatural nature in his rooms. She never said what she was doing in his rooms, except spying. But that line did him no good. What she had found was his battered copy of Krafft-Ebing's *Psychopathia Sexualis*, a textbook from his university days, which he had not opened since a student. Erotica was not of any interest to him. Yet it was enough to bring him to the attention of the Gestapo and their attention was guaranteed to break any man. He admitted finally not only to homosexuality, but named his past lovers as well. Since two of them—Alan and the Viennese politician—were well beyond the heavy sticks of the SS, they concentrated on the others, forgetting to tell Josef that the men he named were already in their custody. He found that out much later, though had he known at the time it would not have relived his guilt. He was sent without further trial to Sachenhausen.

* * *

Sachenhausen. The name does not have the same death knell ring as Dachau or Bergen-Belsen or Auschwitz. But for the prisoners, what they called it did not matter. Thirty kilometers north of Berlin, so conveniently located in the town of Oranienberg, it was an ill-kept secret. Only Josef seemed never to have heard of it. Prisoners were brought there openly by public railway, disembarked at the station, force-marched through three kilometers of residential and factory streets. The local industries used the inmates for hard labor. Everybody knew. Except Josef. Hiding from himself, he hid from the facts, too.

Sachenhausen was a labor camp, not strictly a death camp, and not an extermination camp. The distinction was lost on the 100,000 people who died there. But for Josef that distinction meant a half-life of almost a year's duration in what the president of the people's court, Judge Roland Freisler, called a "recreation home."

The train that Josef was on arrived at the station midday, and the cattle cars opened. Prisoners were hauled out but Josef managed to jump down on his own. His head was still ringing from the beating that had closed one of his eyes, and he thought he heard some horrible chorus of singers. Shaking his head to try and clear it, he only succeeded in making the music louder. It was then he realized that the prisoners were surrounded by a crowd of jeering townsfolk who were half singing, half chanting:

> *Kill the Bromberg murderers!*
> *Vengeance for our brothers in Poland.*
> *Blut fuer blut!*

He turned slowly, theatrically around, raising his hands to them. "But I *am* your brother in Poland!" he cried.

It was the wrong thing to say. One middle aged woman, seeing the pink triangle on his coatsleeve—a present from the Gestapo—aimed a stone at him. "Faggot!" she cried. "Filth!" Her aim was bad and she hit the man standing next to him.

A boy near her, not more than ten years old, was better at it and the stone he shied hit Josef on the arm. "Butt-sticker!" the child cried.

"Don't talk to them. Don't look at them. Run! Run!" It was not a cry of fear but a command from the guards. While the crowd continued, unimpeded, to pelt them with cobblestones and sticks and street filth, the weary prisoners began to stumble forward at a run down the streets.

Later he found out this was the usual greeting given the prisoners by the cultured citizens of Oranienberg. Wars do not make heroes of everyone.

Josef's first glimpse of the camp was of the wooden entrance. But with one eye swollen shut from his interrogation, and perhaps a slight concussion as well, the gates looked twice as tall and fuzzy in their outline. He was by this time no longer running, but rather walking quickly side by side with a man who was clearly a Jehovah's Witness, for he kept up a steady litany of strange prayers.

"Shut up!" Josef suggested, but it only served to make the prayers louder, which in turn served to get them both beaten rather severely several times with the butt of a gun. The Witness said his prayers silently from then on, and Josef was careful to walk a half step ahead and two to the left, just in case. Wars may make heroes of men, but not all the time.

They were herded into a great assembly square under a shock of afternoon sun. Josef was surprised the skies were not weeping for them, then almost laughed at his own fancies, except laughing would have hurt his head and his ribs. He dared a quick glance around with his one good eye. There were signs everywhere and if one read them quickly, they made a kind of perverted sense:

> *THERE IS A ROAD TO FREEDOM.*
> *ITS MILESTONES ARE:*
> *OBEDIENCE, INDUSTRY, HONESTY,*
> *ORDER, CLEANLINESS, SOBRIETY,*

TRUTHFULNESS, SPIRIT OF SACRIFICE AND
LOVE OF FATHERLAND.

A mocking smile played around Josef's mouth. It was hard
not to be obedient and sober when a gun was at your head.
It was hard not to be truthful when a boot was on your
neck. It was hard not to be sacrificed when the other man
was the one in power.

"But I am damned if I am going to love the fatherland
doing it." He must have spoken aloud because too many of
the other prisoners looked quickly at him and moved as
quickly away. Luckily he spoke in Polish, not German. All
he got for speaking aloud was a rifle butt to the stomach.
It knocked his breath away; it did not make him throw up.
He hadn't been allowed to eat for days.

CHAPTER

26

Picture if you can (he said) an enormous semicircle, the outside edge enclosed by an arched stone wall. To one side is a fine barracks with clubhouse and theater and administration building, all for the Gestapo and SS Reserve units. Flowers surround the structures, in pretty formations.

But the center is the roll call area, a place so large fully twenty thousand men—they have to march into it for roll call three times a day whatever their physical condition—are almost lost in it.

Near the roll call area is an isolated barrack. If God had paints, it would be outlined in red. The sign over the door reads *Pathologie*. Not a hospital. No. A place of such ordinary horror that by the time Josef arrived at the camp, its name was never mentioned. You would notice at once the drainage ditches inside. That was necessary where blood flows so freely. And a storeroom for 5,000 corpses. Josef did not believe the number when he was told that first night by the man who lay in the hard bunk by his side.

"That cannot be," he said.

"Everything that goes on here cannot be," the man said, his voice dulled by the dark. "But still it happens."

"Five thousand corpses?" Josef murmured, still not believing. By the first week's end he could name a good many of them.

The prisoners were housed on the other side of the stone wall, far enough away so the Gestapo did not have to look on the eight-six barracks every moment. Here, indeed, was the life of the camp. Each barrack, overfilled already with a hundred people, held three and four hundred, lying head to toe at night like sardines.

And on the far side of the camp were the hothouses full of flowers and vegetables and a hog-breeding farm.

Josef had never paid much attention to flowers before, except for the edelweiss to crown Alan's head, except for roses brought to the theater door. And it seemed odd to him that in this place—where men were routinely castrated, where corpses were dissected and the heads shrunk for experimental purposes, where guards made prisoners roll naked in the snow for hours—that in this place he learned about flowers. Later he could not smell the powerful spice of carnations or the sweet scent of lilac without connecting it with the odor of blood.

Josef quickly learned not to let anyone know he was Polish, because the Poles suffered dreadfully in German hands. For months the guards refused to allow air into the Polish barracks, keeping the doors and windows shut whatever the time of year. Many died at night from suffocation.

He learned not to identify with the Jews, because they too suffered horribly in the camp. They received one-half food rations and were routinely denied any kind of medical attention, until they were corpses. Then the doctors in the *Pathologie* got new heads to shrink.

He learned not to identify with the Gypsies for they were the prime live targets of the *Pathologie* experiments. Dr. Mrugowsky used them as targets for his aconitine nitrate experiment, shooting projectiles into their thighs to prove that it would invariably bring death within two hours. The guards had betting pools on the exact time of those death. *Rom races.*

He was identified as a homosexual, a pink triangle. They were treated terribly enough.

If you had asked Josef Potocki to describe himself before he entered Sachenhausen, he would have said: "I am a Pole educated in Cambridge, a poet and playwright, a member of the minor aristocracy, a man of literate tastes, master of five languages (Polish, German, English, French and Italian), and a gourmet cook." He would never have mentioned sexual preferences. That was no one's business but his own. Besides, he was quite aware of family honor which demanded an heir, an abstract concept he was prepared to deal with in the future.

After Sachenhausen he would have said, "I am a fag." Not gay—there was nothing gay about being a homosexual in that place. Nothing sexual either. Like the other men, he lost all desire for anything but staying alive. The option of "rehabilitation" was tricky. If a night in a brothel proved one could not perform with a prostitute, one would be castrated. Josef preferred to take his chances with the beatings and tortures.

Josef was driftwood, really. He floated through life, making no decisions, no plans. He had drifted into his first love affair in Cambridge, drifted to London and Paris, to Berlin. He had not been able to make plans to leave Germany, and so he had drifted into the hands of the Gestapo. In Sachenhausen he drifted into a plot for escape.

It was in November of 1941, the snow crisp and even on the ground. Josef was lying in his bunk unable to sleep. Outside came the drunken laughter of the German guards as they staggered through the prisoners' barracks. It was clear from their voices that they were standing outside the Jewish huts, for they called out: "Pig-Jews, come out. Out. Now. At once." And he could clearly hear the frantic scrabbling as the Jews in that particular hut came out into the cold in their thin striped pajamas.

"Take off your clothes, and roll," commanded a voice.

Josef had shuddered, knowing what that meant. They were to roll in the snow until the SS men themselves were too cold to stand about watching any more. Then the Jews would be allowed to crawl back into their unheated huts and try to get warm under their thin blankets. Many would be dead in days of pneumonia coupled with despair.

Though he had heard of this, he had never actually seen it and something seemed to force him to get up, to walk to the door of the barracks, to open it a crack.

"Josef!" Someone whispered his name, put a hand on his arm. "It is nothing. We can do nothing. Do not make a fuss."

He turned abruptly, started to say something aloud, something about being men, about fighting, about dying with honor, something theatrical. A hand was slapped brutally over his mouth, his arms were pinned behind him.

"Do nothing. When they are gone, we will be gone, too. We will kill you if you ruin our plan." The words were whispered fiercely in his ear.

He nodded and the hand dropped from his mouth. He whispered back: "Take me." He did not know the plan. He did not know the planners. He did not care. "Take me." They might kill him anyway. He did not care. He was driftwood, you see.

When the drunken soldiers had had enough of the game—"Jesus, Maria—it is too cold for this. I want some more schnappes," one complained—and the last of the Jews had crawled back inside the hut, someone in the dark tapped Josef on the shoulder.

"Come," a voice muffled by the night told him. "You can be the lookout. Karol is at the last minute too frightened. Better the devil you know . . ."

He went with them, not knowing either the plan or the direction, not knowing that Karol had already informed on them, that Karol was a spy who was neither a fag nor a

Pole, but a Czech jailed for profiteering. They slipped out through the trap door in the ceiling, by the chimney, the door that was supposed to be sealed shut. He never found out who had opened it. They clambered down the sides of the building. Josef was told to come last, to watch, to call out any warnings.

The guards were waiting for them, counting them and naming them, just as Karol had listed. But Josef, still on the roof, crouched by the stovepipe chimney as the lookout, was neither expected nor counted. And when the others were marched away to the *Pathologie*, a welcome addition to Dr. Mrugowsky's dwindling supply of experimental prisoners, Josef shivered in his thin striped pajamas by the chimney and tried to plan his retreat. But the trapdoor was shut again, either frozen by the cold or bolted from inside by the informer Karol. So once more Josef drifted.

Pleased with the night's catch, the guards began to drink riotously in their own warm barracks. Josef practically strolled up to the fence and, heedless of cuts to his hands and feet, flung himself up and over the wire.

By morning's light, he was in a forest somewhere—he was never to be sure where—outside of Oranienberg, colder than he had ever been in the camp, his hands cramped and stiff, his nose running ceaselessly, a line of diarrhea brought on by fright hardening on the inside of his right thigh. But free.

He would have frozen in that filthy condition had not a woodcutter discovered him just as the sun was rising.

The woodcutter was Henrik R—, also known as The Rat. He was a partisan.

CHAPTER

27

Forget every romantic notion you have ever had about the partisans (he said) for they are all incorrect. These were not brave men and women brilliantly plotting moves against the sluggish enemy. These were not the underground chess game masters checkmating the Reich. These were farmers and woodcutters and escapees. These were students and housewives and professional thieves. These were the flotsam and jetsam of the world, driftwood like Josef, whose victories were sometimes catastrophes, whose defeats were the stuff of legends.

Some of them were heroes.

Some of them were fools.

All of them were liars because they were afraid or because they were brave or because they could not care or because they cared too much.

Once he was no longer starving, no longer freezing, no longer running from the Sachenhausen Gestapo, Josef joined the particular cell that The Rat led. He did not like the woodcutter, who was a rough, unlettered boor. But Henrik made him feel safe, for the first time in years. He became a partisan because he was grateful and because he was afraid and because like any piece of driftwood, he went where the tide pulled. If Henrik had wanted to make love to him, he would have assented; if Henrik had beaten him, he would have blessed the striking hand.

At night, deep in the forest in lean-tos Henrik showed them how to build—but without fires to give their positions away—the five men and three women of Henrik's group told little stories of the resistance to lend themselves courage.

One, a Jewish university student who had fled to the woods under cover of a terrible storm while being transported to Dachau, reported to them of the diarists in Warsaw, the "Joy of Sabbath" circle that recorded the news of any who fought back. "One mother," he recalled, "fought like a lioness." He had repeated the word several times and the women nodded, echoing him.

"A lioness," they said.

"She refused to turn her baby over to the murderers as they asked."

"A lioness," said one woman, herself a mother whose children had all died on a forced march. She called herself Mutter Holle.

"And what happened?" Josef asked.

The student shook his head. "They grabbed the child from her and hurled it from the window. But . . ." he turned a ravaged face towards Josef and there was a shining in it, a reflection of borrowed courage, "but *she did not turn the baby over to them on her own.*"

Josef did not speak but made a *tsach* with his tongue against his teeth.

Mutter Holle put her hand on Josef's arm. "You think, then, it did not matter, that the results were the same. But you are wrong, Prince." They called him Prince because of his manner and because the student had known something of the Potocki family, being a Pole himself. "But we are all stronger for such women."

Josef did not know what to say. He was thinking: a dead child is a dead child. There is nothing good that comes of murdering a baby. But he had seen so much horror in his year at Sachenhausen, he dreamt at night that drains in his body were constantly filling with blood, though when he had been in the camp he had only dreamed of food. He said nothing and the women took it for agreement.

"Josef understands," Mutter Holle said. "He is a Prince."

Only once did Henrik speak to them of the resistance as a movement. "We have not come here to live," he said, pointing to the forest around them. "We have not come here to stay alive. It is our sacred duty to fight when we can and to die if we must, but to avenge what they have done to our Germany." Then having delivered himself of the only beautiful paragraph he was likely ever to utter, Henrik finished in rather more usual fashion, "The shits. We will kill them all."

Josef did not remind him that of the eight of them, only four were actually German—Henrik, Mutter Holle, and the two men, brothers, who had escaped conscription into the army: Fritz and Franz, known as Donner and Blitzen.

Josef lived with the Oranienberg partisans in the forest for the four months of winter: November, December, January, and February. And in all that time—except for a raid on a grocery in the outskirts of Oranienberg for much-needed supplies, and three late-night forays onto the train tracks to destroy sections of it that were built back again the next day by concentration camp inmates—they did nothing except exchange stories.

In March, the little band finally planned a real raid. Henrik told them of a storage depot on the other side of Berlin, and even drew a map to show them how they could fan out and then meet again safely.

"We have only four guns," Josef pointed out.

"We have courage," said Mutter Holle.

"They are shits," Henrik said. "If necessary we will kill them with our bare hands." He said it in his growl of a voice but Josef noted with some detachment that he did not offer to give up his own gun.

And so the plan was set. The guns were in the hands of those who knew how to use them—Henrik, Donner, Blitzen, and Josef who, as a boy, had often gone hunting on his stepfather's estate. He did not tell them that he had never actually killed anything on those trips, except once a wood pigeon, and that by accident. The blood on his hands as he tried to breathe life back into the little grey bird had made the gameskeeper and his stepfather laugh.

Those without guns—the three women and the Jew, who was, after all, a student and a rabbi—carved spears out of branches, making the points as sharp as Henrik's knife.

In their layers of cast-off clothing, makeshift weapons in hand, they looked less like a band of partisans than a pleistocene hunting party out after sabertooth. But Henrik's fierce leadership sustained them. "They are shits," was the war party's hunting cry.

The outcome of the raid was never in doubt. They all expected to die, though not a one of them said it aloud. They revived the old resistance stories: the mothers who would not give their children over to the Nazis, the rabbis who rushed onto the points of the bayonets screaming the Shema, the partisan who threw himself in front of a bus as a diversion so his comrades could escape. They filled themselves with such stories, never mentioning that all the stories ended in death.

Josef alone said it. "We are all going to die."

They shunned him then. They literally turned their backs on him though he was telling no more and no less than the truth they all knew. From the moment he said what was in their secret hearts, he no longer existed for them. Henrik took his gun away and gave it to one of the women. She kept her spear as well. So Josef alone went into that final battle against the storage depot without a weapon.

Because of it—who says that God does not have a sense of humor?—he alone was not killed.

* * *

The storage depot was not one building but three great silos. Henrik's plan had been simple; he had drawn it with a stick on the muddy ground. Those with guns would be in the forefront, those without guns behind. They would rush the small wooden house in which the depot manager lived, take him prisoner, find something with which to blow up the silos, and escape.

"Melt back into the woods," Henrik said.

When Josef asked how they might expect to find something to blow up the silos with, no one answered. He had become a non-person, his questions not worth answering. And he understood, then, that the point of their raid was not to blow up anything at all. The point was to die so that they, in turn, could become stories for other partisans to tell around the fires that were not fires.

So when Henrik and Donner and Blitzen and the woman called Nadia went forward with their guns, followed closely by the rabbi, Mutter Holle and the third woman, who had rabbity teeth and was called Hexe—witch—Josef stayed behind. He was not afraid. Having lived a year in Sachenhausen, having managed through four months in the woods, he had no fear left. But he did not want to die for someone else's story. If he had to die, he wanted to die for his own.

He watched them cut down by machine gun fire, for Henrik had not mentioned, perhaps had not even known, that there were guards atop the silos. He watched and he did not even weep for them. He knew that when he told their story a day or a month or a year from then, then he would cry.

He went back into the woods, found the last of their meager supplies, broke off a walking stick for himself which, without Henrik's knife, he could not sharpen as a weapon, and began to go due east: towards the rising sun, towards the border that was no longer a border, towards Poland, towards home.

CHAPTER

28

It is difficult to believe (he said) that Josef P. made it to his stepfather's estate alive and unharmed. But the war was filled with such unbelievable stories. This man hid in the cupboard of his neighbor's house the entire war. That one was killed out walking his dog. This woman missed her train and it was blown up. That woman begged a ride and was murdered. This child lived safely three years in the woods. That one had its brains slammed against the camp's stone wall. There is nothing that is not believable in this world. Josef P. came home.

He walked into the house to find Potocki dead, taken for a conspirator and shot in the gameskeeper's hut where he had so often gutted rabbits and skinned deer. His mother, still beautiful, was mistress to the commandant who had set up his headquarters in the house. Josef stopped only to take a few possessions—some fresh clothing, a backpack of food, a passport with an extra photograph, a knife, his stepfather's prized hunting rifle and extra bullets—he was no fool after all. These were given to him by his old nurse, who also cut his hair and trimmed his nails and let him sleep till nightfall in her own bed, his head resting on her breasts as if he were still a child and not a man. He did not see his mother.

"Take your father's ring," the old nurse had said, putting his stepfather's ring in his hand.

"This is Potocki's ring," Josef said, looking at the crest and the entwined letters.

"He was your true father," she said. "You are his true son."

"My mother?"

"Ah, poor lamb, no better than she should have been. But the old man . . ." and by this she meant the first husband, whom Josef had always believed was his father, ". . . the old man was a beast. Unnatural. Her true love was Potocki. And you were of that union indeed." She kissed him and sent him into the night. He never was to know whether that story was, like all her stories told to him late at night, a fairy tale or real. His mother died near the war's end, her beautiful golden hair shaved off, hanged by the local partisans as a collaborator. He never saw her again.

The woods around his stepfather's estate were well known to him and he planned to stay there throughout the war, for everyone said it would not be a prolonged seige. The Germans would never stand up to the combined might of the world, not to the revenge of the Poles. So his old nurse had told him; so he now chose to believe. Forgetting Sachenhausen and the tales he had heard. Forgetting the deaths he had already seen. Clean clothes, a fresh haircut, food in the belly—they are great convincers. Josef was tired of death. He dreamed of peace. He dreamed of sleep.

He woke up surrounded by men.

The sun was already overhead and streaming down in bright ribbands through the trees. At first all he could see were the shadows of men bending over him, elongated, black, backlit, menacing. Then one moved closer and he could make out a face, an angel's face haloed in gold curls. For a moment he thought he had died and was in heaven and Alan had found him again. Then the angel pulled him roughly to a sitting position and Josef saw he looked nothing like Alan, the gold curls being only a trick of the light behind. He had brown hair with gold high-lights and his nose was slightly beaked. His eyes were the dark mud of the Vistula in flood.

"Who are you?" he asked Josef in Polish, then in German.

Caution, never an old habit, suddenly claimed Josef. He answered in Polish. "I am called . . . Prince."

"He looks like one," a man commented. "Those clothes."

"Don't be stupid. What would a prince . . ."

"They shot the old one."

"Is he the son?"

"The mother is a collaborator."

"We should kill him now."

"Wait." It was the boy. He knelt beside Josef and pushed up Josef's left sleeve.

"What are you doing?" Josef asked.

"Looking for a number," the boy said. "To see if you are a spy or an escapee."

"There were no numbers in Sachenhausen."

The boy sat back on his heels. "So . . . a Jew?" He spoke rapidly in a language Josef did not know, though he guessed it was Hebrew.

Josef shook his head.

"You do not have the look of a Rom."

He shook his head again. "I am a Pole. I am . . . a fag-got. A 175er. A . . ."

The boy stood. "He would not admit to that if he were a German."

"Why not?" The speaker was a heavy-faced man, his beard growing in black and white clumps. "All Germans are secret fags. If he *is* a fag, he is just telling us he is a German. And you know what fags are: liars and blabber-mouths, incapable of loyalty."

"That," Josef said, finally standing and looking straight

at the man, "is exactly what Himmler said. Perhaps *you* are the secret German spy."

The man hit him and Josef went down like a stone.

The boy knelt beside him again, but he was laughing, a lyrical, pure laugh. Joseph had not heard such laughter in years. There seemed to be no cynicism in it. None at all. "No German spy would be so inept," the boy said, helping Josef to his feet once more. "I say we keep him."

"He will be the death of us all," the bearded man warned.

Secretly Josef agreed with him, if past history were any indicator.

And that is how he fell in with a group of Jewish partisans.

There were thirteen in all. The boy—who was no boy at all but twenty-three—was called The Avenger, for his entire family had been burned alive in their synagogue and he alone, away at medical school, had been spared.

The bearded man was known as Rebbe though, as far as Josef was concerned, he was the least holy man he had ever met: foul-mouthed and quick to judge.

There were three brothers known as The Hammer, The Anvil and The Rod who rarely spoke, except to each other. There was a thin, dark Russian aesthete who answered to Ivan the Terrible and who had carved a tiny chess set out of oak, with acorn chessmen. He had played the game by himself until Josef arrived and then, after Josef won their third game together, he never played again. There were actually two women, known as Shuttle and Reed—though in all the weeks Josef was with them he never was able to tell which was which. They stayed to themselves and always slept apart from the men, their arms about one another. They might have been sisters, with the same square jaws, green eyes, blue-black curly hair cut short, large peasant hands. They might even have been mother and daughter, though Josef couldn't have said which was the older.

There were five men in their sixties, grey-haired and grey-bearded, who had come from the same village. Woodcutters, they had been away deep in the woods when the Germans had arrived. On their return they had found their families slaughtered, their homes looted and burned. "Even the gold wedding ring on my wife's finger was gone," one said. "Along with the finger." He did not say it sadly or angrily or with any emotion at all. It was as if he were reciting an old old story told to him so long ago, it had lost its power to shock or wound. Four of the men had taken the names of trees: Oak, Ash, Rowan, Birch. But the fifth, who was their leader, called himself Holz-Wadel because that was the forestmen's name for the full moon, a time when felling of trees was at its height. "I fell only German trees," he said. Again, without emotion.

They were on their way to the outskirts of Lublin. There, almost in sight of the city, was a new death camp: Majdanek it was called. It had been started the previous December and was filled with Russian soldiers—prisoners of war. It was Holz-Wadel's idea—and supported by other partisan groups they had come in contact with—that if they could liberate at least some of the camp, their ranks would swell with men who had been trained as fighters.

Josef nodded his head. It was at least a plan, so unlike the sort of stories and silly dreams that Henrik and his crew had been about. "Take me," he said.

They were all practiced woodsmen, the women, too: careful, quiet and strong. It would have been hard to tell where one had traveled through the forest, much less fourteen, and Josef reveled in their company. The stories they traded at night had nothing to do with resistance and horror, nothing to do with the many awful ways of dying. They told one another the old stories: the woodcutters recounted the folk tales of their mountains; the Avenger being closest of them all to childhood, the nursery stories his mother had told him; Rebbe, true to his name if not his nature, recalling stories from the Old Testament. The Russian aesthete told Russian stories in verse, translating them for the others in a voice made high with emotion.

When it was his turn, Josef began by reciting English ballads like Sir Patrick Spens and The Wife of Usher's Well. He ignored his old favorites—Schiller and Goethe— judging that his audience might guess his choice of German poets meant more than simple admiration. They were still unsure of him. He was the only non-Jew. But his training in the theater stood him in good stead, and he soon became their favorite entertainment. He ran through the early English poets and then remembered pieces of Dante for good measure, though the portions of the *Inferno* proved too dark and too real for them. When he translated "Abandon All Hope . . ." the two women put their hands up over their ears and began to weep silently. Josef stopped, watching them in fascination. He had never seen anyone weep without a sound. When he mentioned it the next morning to the boy, he was told they had learned to weep that way in one of the camps, so as not to be noticed. The Avenger did not tell him which camp. Josef did not ask.

And so they came, by slow, cautious stages, to the outskirts of Lublin. There they joined up with a larger group of partisans in the woods but were warned that Majdanek was too well guarded. The stories of death began again; they told them like beads on a rosary. The Shuttle and the Reed left Josef's group then, for there were other women who took them in. And Ivan the aesthete, tired of life in the woods, was given false papers and sent on his way through the various undergrounds towards the west, a trip which sent him doubling back along some of the same trails they had just traveled. They heard months later, rumor piled upon rumor, that he had been killed near Paris, captured and tortured but refusing to give out any names.

"Who would have thought the bastard had it in him," was the Rebbe's terse comment. As it seemed an appropriate enough obituary, no one said anything more.

But Josef thought about Ivan's death, doubting he, himself, could have held out in silence. After all, hadn't he given the names of all his lovers, living and dead? Hadn't he held back in the raid when Henrik and Donner and Blitzen and Nadia and the rabbi and Mutter Holle and the Hexe had all gone down under the rain of the Nazi guns? Then, unable to bear thinking any more about his failures, he thought instead of Paris, remembering it as it had been when he had lived there: the small cafes, the busy streets, the life that had been so quietly purposeless and so full of hope.

He was still trying to sort it all out when they broke into groups of sixes and sevens and eights and began, over a period of a month, an active campaign of sabotage against strategic railway lines and storage depots.

"Always railway lines and storage depots," he muttered once.

"Those bastards don't shoot back," the Rebbe answered.

Josef did not mention how his earlier companions had died. He concentrated instead on their stealthy incursions, on the feel of a steel pry under the tracks.

And one night, the tracks they worked on were the ones that led to the little town of Chelmno, by the Narew River.

It was in June.

CHAPTER

29

How does one become a man of honor (he asked); how does one redeem a life? Think of Oskar Schindler. He was a gambler, a womanizer, a drunk, a profiteer, a Nazi. His life was spelled out in one dishonor after another. Yet he saved 1,200 people. The Jews he saved said, "Among the unjust, we do not forget the just."

Just so, a piece of driftwood like Josef P. became a hero.

Unlike Auschwitz, Dachau, Bergen-Belsen, the camp at Chelmno was a secret. Even the Jews of the Lodz ghetto who were sent there by the thousands, even the entire Jewish population of the Warthegau killed there did not fear the name. They had never heard it. Chelmno has no national survivor organizations. No one survived. Two men only escaped; two men were found there alive at the war's end. Four men. And one woman. Księżniczka.

A rumor came to Josef's group from the Warsaw ghetto partisans. But it was rumor only. It was said there was an extermination camp fifty kilometers from Lodz. The rumor was horrible enough. Yet they had all seen horror. They were men and women who had been tortured, who had numbers burned in their arms, who had buried their butchered babies or seen them thrown into a fire, who had been in a building where the drains ran red with human blood. Of course they *believed* the rumor. They just did not know what they could do.

"We will blow up the tracks to Powiercie." Holz-Wadel offered his one solution, running his fingers through his thick grey hair. The rumor had said prisoners were brought into that town, then marched down the dusty road to Zawadki where they spent the night in a large unheated mill building.

"We will blow up the mill," argued Rebbe, hawking up a big glob of phlegm and deliberately missing Josef's boot by the space of a finger. "We could rush the Nazi bastards there." But the rumor had also said that in Zawadki there were SS barracks.

"We could dynamite the SS barracks," said Avenger. "If we had enough dynamite. If we dared." But he said it with a grin to show that even he thought it was a terrible idea. His smile was so infectious, a small laugh ran around the circle of plotters.

"The *schloss*," said Ash, and the tree brothers agreed with him. The rumor said that it was in a *schloss*, a castle, that the prisoners were held.

But Josef shook his head vigorously and threw his hat on the ground. "We want to live, not die. We want to save people, not be martyrs. Yes?" He spoke directly to Rebbe, but he meant it for them all. And he spoke with such ardor, they all nodded their heads: yes, yes, yes.

"Then we must follow where they take the prisoners, and rescue who is left alive." For the final part of the rumor said that this was a camp on wheels. *On wheels*. They did not know what that meant, but they meant to find out.

That night, and without further preparation, three men— Birch, Ash, and Avenger—went to watch the trains come into Powiercie. Three men—Rowan, Rebbe and Holz-Wadel—went to scout the mill building. Three men—the brothers Hammer, Anvil, and Rod—went to check on the SS barracks. And one man—Josef, because he was not

Jewish, because he spoke both Polish and German with an aristocratic accent—actually went into the town of Chelmno, called Kulmhof by the Germans, to see what he could find out.

The brothers never returned. If they were captured, if they were tortured, they surely gave nothing away. But they were gone as if they had never been. So it was with this war.

The others met back in the woods three nights later to report.

"The trains are heavily guarded, soldiers everywhere," said Birch.

"The mill likewise," Rebbe said. "Bastards!" He spit on the ground, but this time away from Josef.

For a moment they were silent, thinking about the SS barracks, thinking about the brothers and their fate, wondering if they were alive, believing that they were dead, willing still to wait but expecting nothing. So it was with everyone Josef had met in the camps, in the woods. One day a man was there, the next he was not. He did not even have any more tears.

"What of the town?" Holz-Wadel asked, the sentence even in his mouth, without emotion, without fear, almost without hope. Almost.

"The town," Josef said, and for a moment stopped. What could he say? It was nothing, that town. Small, insignificant, a single road through it and mud-colored. A church, a fine house for the teacher, a ruined castle surrounded by high wooden walls festooned with barbed wire. And Nazis everywhere.

"I hitched a ride with a local man, on his hay cart. His horse was as old as he, and with probably as few teeth. He was quite talkative."

"The horse?" Avenger asked, but he winked at Josef to share the joke.

"The horse had little to say, but the man spoke like an ass. A horse pulling an ass," Josef said. The others laughed.

"I told him I was a Potocki and he pulled his forelock.
He asked if I was traveling home, and I agreed. To see my
mother, I told him. He had a cousin who had once seen
my mother, he said, on her way to a ball. Or maybe it was
my grandmother. A fine woman. A handsome woman, he
said, if he could be allowed the compliment. I said he
could."

"Ah, the aristocracy . . ." Rebbe said. This time he did
not spit.

"Then the old man looked at the road and gave a little
slap with the reins as if that could urge the old horse on.
'The Jews,' he said mumbling between widely spaced
teeth, 'they are like leeches on a wound. Better to salt
them down.' "

The woodcutters grumbled at this.

"I did not say it—he did," Josef said. "But I asked him
how that salt was to be applied. And he told me that it was
to be done directly. There. In Chelmno. And he was glad
of it. 'How directly?' I asked. And he said the Jews of the
Warthegau were being brought by freight trains to the
Kolo junction, transferred to another train on the narrow-
gauge track, and proceeding to Powiercie."

"Maybe we could dynamite the tracks *between* Kolo and
Powiercie," mused Holz-Wadel, but the others ignored him.

"He said that transports from the ghetto came in special
twelve-car trains from Lodz."

"We saw one, then," Birch interrupted.

"Yes—twelve cars," Ash added. "We counted."

"And over a hundred police accompanying it," Avenger
put in.

"That's what the old man said." Josef nodded. "A special unit."

"For an ass, he certainly brayed a lot." Rebbe hawked
up, thought better of it, and swallowed his spit.

"What of the town?" Holz-Wedel prompted again, and
again without emotion, neither impatience nor anger.

"They came by van to the *schloss*," Josef said. "This I
saw myself. Through the gates. I could not get closer."

"And the old man? What did he say about them once they are inside?" asked the boy, putting his hand on Josef's arm.

Josef was silent for a long moment, remembering. When he spoke, his voice was low, on the verge of a whisper. "He said that they go in and they come out but it is not the same. And he laughed. I laughed with him. We had a good laugh at those Jews." His arm was trembling under the boy's hand. "I saw several men walking, their ankles in chains. I pointed at them. We had another laugh."

"And the town?" Holz-Wedel said.

"It is small and full of SS men. The vans that take the Jews from the *schloss* head out of town, towards a forest. I did not go there nor show any interest in it. It would have been too suspicious. The old man and I laughed all the way through Chelmno, about the Jews, about the Gypsies, about social deviants, about fags. How we laughed. He admired the crest of my ring. I laughed and said farewell. He would have invited me to his home to meet his wife but I was afraid I might murder him in his kitchen. I said my mother was expecting me and the one thing she would not tolerate is that I be late. He nodded. He understood."

"Towards a forest . . ." mused Holz-Wedel, and there was the tiniest bit of emotion in his voice.

They circled carefully through the woods towards the far side of Chelmno. It took them three nights traveling, three days hidden in carefully dug trenches, the tops overlaced with branches. They were taking no chances. They came at last, round and about, to the edge of the forest. Up to twenty feet away were alfalfa fields, the purple flowers moving sluggishly in a puzzling wind. There were several hutches at the field's end, and they could see three men and a boy of about thirteen shuffling along, feeding the rabbits. To the right was the Narew River, meandering slowly. They kept their heads down, for flat-bottomed boats were occasionally poled along.

The guards seemed quiet and they had no dogs, which Josef at least was thankful for. He had no wish to shoot a dog, though he had no compunction about shooting the guards if he had to. So far had he come in his two years of war.

They waited several hours, before Holz-Wedel said what they were all thinking. "This is not yet where the vans go." He disappeared quietly into the deeper woods, the others following.

Josef watched the shuffling men at the rabbit hutch for a moment more and saw how they seemed to watch over the boy, though not one of them touched him. Then he, too, went back into the deep woods.

That night they circled even further away from Chelmno and by morning were in place, crouched on the edge of another clearing. The sun came up and the birds sang their hearts out, as if the world were as sweet and pure as the first morning of God's paradise. Later Josef would know the name of the wood: Rzuchow. That first sunrise it seemed like Eden.

Then a group of thirty-five men in an open truck arrived and when they got out at the far edge of the field, they shuffled in a manner that made Josef know at once that these were prisoners. They stood still, as if waiting, but unlike most people in a group anticipating an event, they did not move about or talk or even slap at flies. They were as still as statues and, in the golden sunlight, looked made of bronze. Only the truck driver and the guard with him spoke, slapping one another on the back twice in the course of their conversation.

There was a moment of complete silence—guards and birds simultaneously quieting—and Josef could suddenly hear a strange, low rumbling. If later he remembered that rumble as the sound of the Wild Hunt, it was only a fancy on his part. For within minutes the rumbling turned into three large vans, like furniture-moving vans, about six by three meters. The outsides of the vans were covered with narrow overlapping boards, and with the sun glinting off the sides, he thought at first that they were armored. It was only later he realized they were merely wood painted a dark grey.

"Why such vans here?" Avenger whispered to him, and Josef had no answer. The old man had said nothing about them.

Then the vans stopped and the shackled men shambled to the back. One man strained for a moment at each door and the nearer van's doors suddenly flew open and a naked woman tumbled out onto the ground.

A small moan ran around the watching men in the forest but Josef silenced them by lifting his hand. In the few seconds the moan and the ensuing silence took, three more bodies had fallen from the back of the truck.

Every two hours the vans arrived in the clearing and all Josef and his comrades could do was squat behind the dark trees at the forest's edge and witness the horror of the events, for the vans were escorted by scores of SS vehicles. The partisans were vastly outnumbered and outgunned.

When they saw the first bodies tumble out, they were angry. But when that woman was followed by another and another and another—eighty-two people in all pulled, dragged, and rolled out of the van—they were numb. And though they could not see clearly from behind the trees, they found out soon enough that the corpses had been mangled for the gold in their teeth and then rolled into an enormous mass grave there in the field by the grey Narew.

Once the three vans had been emptied, off they were driven again toward Chelmno, leaving the shackled workers and their guards behind. Every two hours they returned with another full load.

That first day Josef and his friends watched from sunup to sundown, seven trips for the vans, three vans each time, twenty-one loads. Josef did the arithmetic for them. "Between eighty and one hundred dead each time means they have killed over eighteen hundred to almost two thousand men and women and children today alone. It is worse than Sachenhausen." He had thought nothing could be worse.

The men did not respond to his mathematics, but simply moved swiftly back into the deep woods.

That night, by mutual consent, they said nothing. They did not even plan for the morning. But Josef could hear one man or another weeping far into the night. Near midnight, Rebbe came to him. He did not speak but handed Josef a bottle of cognac. Josef did not ask how he had come by such a treasure, he just drank fully a quarter of the bottle straight before the man took it from him and left him alone. It was then he thought of Alan, whom he had never thought of in Sachenhausen or in the six years since his desertion.

"'Tis a far, far better thing," he quoted to himself with great passion, meaning it was better to go down fighting in a border dispute, better to be cut down in a hail of bullets on a raid, than to be gassed in a six-meter van, fighting eighty relatives and friends for a last breath of air. Better to be a resistance legend than to be thrown away like an old rag into a vast, unmarked grave.

In the morning they returned to the forest's edge. It was as if they could not believe what they had seen the day before, that they had to see it again for it to be real. And so for a second day, this one overcast with a sky as grey as the river, they counted vans. Eight trips this time, despite the threatening weather, and the addition of a round of machine gun fire.

"They have shot the shackled prisoners," Rowan said. He had the best eyes. "There are to be no witnesses."

By evening the field was totally deserted and they chanced going across it. Not all of them and not all at once. The boy, Birch, and Josef drew the short straws and went first. They ran warily, bent over, and Josef kept turning to stare at the river growing blacker every minute, but they were alone in the harrowing field.

They came to the side of the pit in the deepening dark. It was enormous, full of shadows: shadows of arms, of legs, of heads thrown back, mouths open in silenced screams. Lines of Dante ran through Josef's mind but, he realized, not even the great Alighieri could touch the horror of what lay at his feet. The smell—a lingering fog of exhaust fumes, the stench of loosened bowels, the sweet-sickly odor of the two- and three-day dead—drenched them.

Josef stared down at the bodies, but only one in the thousands did he really see—a child, no more than three or four, fair-haired, on the very top of the heap. Its thumb was firmly in its mouth, like a stopper.

He wept.

They all three wept, loudly and unashamedly.

Then Avenger cried out, "Look! Someone is moving!"

At first Josef thought it must be because of the dark, because of the shadows, because of their fear. Then he had an even darker thought that the gasses bodies exude when decomposing must be rising from the earlier dead. But Avenger was, after all, a medical student and surely he would know all that. Besides, he had already leaped down into that hellish pit, pushing the stiffening bodies aside. And when he stood up again, shakily, on the backs and breasts and sides of slaughtered people, he held a single body in his arms.

It was a young woman and, even in the quickening dark, Josef could see that her arm was moving sluggishly, that her face had an odd pattern of roses on the cheeks.

Avenger handed up the body to Josef and Birch helped the boy climb out himself. But by that time the girl had stopped moving, had even stopped breathing. Josef could feel her die in his arms. So he laid her down on the ground and, putting his mouth on hers, the taste of vomit bitter on his lips, he tried to give her breath.

They took turns trying to revive her, Avenger using the medical school method, lifting her arms up and down and, when he was tired, Josef breathing into her mouth. And it was into Josef's mouth that she, at last, sputtered and coughed. By the time she was able to breathe on her own, the field was completely dark. There was no moon. There were no stars. They could all have been dead and in the pit for all that they could see.

The girl did not speak, did not say her name, did not ask where she was or who they were. She only put her hand to her head as if it ached, as if she were dizzy and could not stand. So Avenger took off his jacket and wrapped it tenderly around her. Then he picked her up and carried her, as if she were a child, going unerringly back to the woods, though there was no light to see by. Josef and Birch followed them into that darker dark.

In the morning she was still alive, still silent, though the roses no longer bloomed so brightly on her cheeks. Her body was stained with feces and vomit, her own and that of the other victims. Her red hair was matted and tangled. There were three scratches on her face and neck, and one on her left leg. Occasionally she coughed up phlegm and then, embarrassed, turned and spat it on the ground.

Avenger gave her his jacket and Birch his shirt. When she tried to return one or the other, they shook their heads and Avenger smiled that tender smile of his. She buttoned the jacket carefully over the shirt, and the tails hung below the jacket and half down her thighs.

The next night, flushed with the victory of her life, and the night after as well, they went back to the pit, sorting through the stiffening bodies, trying to find someone else alive. The girl stayed behind in the protection of the dark forest.

Though they found two men and one woman who were still breathing, the men both died, raving, in the forest before morning. It was, Avenger, explained to them, a normal complication of such gassing. The woman lived till noon the next day, wrapped in Josef's coat. She complained of starbursts, of shadows moving towards her.

Before she died, she told them how she had come to
Chelmno, her voice never rising above a hoarse whisper,
as if it had already died. Later the men pieced together her
story. She spoke of the castle—the *schloss*, she called
it—a manor house with an old granary and two wooden
huts. She and her family had been brought by train from
the Lodz ghetto, then by truck, into the *schloss* courtyard.
There they had been reassured by a handsome German
commandant, in passable Polish, that they were only going
to a work camp.

"Only a place to work where our labor would help the
German fatherland," she whispered, then pointed. "See the
shadows." But there were none.

So they needed to wash, the commandant had told them
and while they washed their clothing would be disinfected
from the long and horrible ride. Those had been his words,
such words of comfort, "the long and horrible ride." They
had to disrobe, therefore, and put their valuables, their papers, and other items of identification like lockets and
rings, in baskets especially marked with their names.

"Then we went into the cellar at the *schloss*," she whispered hoarsely. "I held my little daughter's hand. We were
both so embarrassed being naked in front of strangers.
Even naked in front of family members. It is not done, you
know. It is not done." Her eyes filled with tears. "I would
have picked up my child, but she said 'No, Mama. Not
skin on skin.' So I held her hand and read the signs out
loud to her as we walked down the hall. *To the washroom*
said one sign over a stairway. *To the Doctor* another. I told
her not to be afraid. Oh . . ." She had silently then, whispering through the tears, "that I had held her that one last
time."

She told them that all the prisoners were sent down the
stairs and to an enclosed ramp that led into a van. They
had to run from the blows the Germans had suddenly begun to rain upon their heads. Almost one hundred people
had been crammed in.

"My little daughter was buried in the crush," she said.

"I heard her cry out once, and then not again. I came the very last into our van and the doors slammed after me. The floor was of tin and latticed. It hurt my bare feet. We were all screaming, crying out. I called my daughter's name over and over and over but she did not answer. Then the van started up and that is all I can remember."

They did not tell her that everyone else in the van was dead, dead from the exhaust piped in, dead in the crush of so many people scrabbling for air, or dead from a final bullet in the brain. They did not have to.

Later that morning, just before she died, she cried out the name "Rachel." Josef knew—they all knew even without being told—that it was her daughter's name. They buried her there, in the woods, with a simple stone to mark the place. Josef stood with the others around the grave.

"There are only eight of us," Holz-Wadel said, "And one is not a Jew. Not enough for a real minyan."

"Nine," the girl said suddenly. "And God will not care." It was the first time she had spoken. She joined them, hugging herself.

Josef was not sure if she meant God would not care whether they had the proper number of men for the funeral or that if she meant He simply no longer cared about anyone at all. He did not ask.

After they realized she could speak, they questioned her: what was her name, where had she come from, who had been with her.

She shook her head. "I do not know."

Avenger took her hand in his. "You mean you do not remember." He was worried. He knew that gas poisoning brought psychoses, brought deterioration of personality.

She shook her head. "I do not know. I have no memories in my head but one."

"What one?" Holz-Wadel asked.

"A fairy tale."

"Mishuganah!" Rebbe said, shaking his head and walking off.

"What fairy tale?" Josef asked.

She shrugged. "I do not know its name. But in it I am a princess in a castle and a great mist comes over us. Only I am kissed awake. I know now that there is a castle and it is called 'the *schloss*.' But I do not know for sure if that is *my* castle. I only remember the fairy tale and it seems, somehow, that it is my story as well."

"She means 'Sleeping Beauty in the Wood,' " Josef said.

The woodcutters nodded and Avenger smiled, almost as if he were simultaneously amused and charmed. And relieved.

"Then we will call you Princess," Josef said. "Princess Briar Rose, after the story." But he used the Polish word: *Księżniczka*.

CHAPTER

30

"Ein Tag-ein tausend," (he said). It was something Josef heard years later from his friend, the priest of Chelmno. That was what the guards used to say to one another, and to the people of the town: *"Ein Tag-ein tausend."* It means *One day—one thousand*, the numbers of people to be killed. A tally stick. A rota.

But Josef and his comrades had saved one. One in a thousand. And they knew their chances of saving one more were slim. And dangerous.

"We must get her away," Josef said to them. "We must find her clothes. Shoes. Real food."

"Oxygen if we can," added Avenger.

Clothes and shoes and food were possible. For oxygen she would have to breathe the air. They all knew that. They had been eating mushrooms and berries and many greens that the woodcutters knew were safe. They had caught fish from the Narew, but eaten them raw, not willing to chance a fire. They themselves wore old clothes, old shoes. Josef remembered a pair of boots he had given to a servant because they had not fit properly. What he would have given for those boots now. He dreamed at night of the *gateau* he had eaten with Alan in Paris. Or Vienna. Or

Berlin. He was no longer sure. He didn't dream of Alan, just of the cake. One morning he had awakened, certain he smelled coffee.

"Food first," Josef said to them. "And shoes next." He was surprised when they agreed, when they asked for his advice. Somehow, by breathing life into the girl, by naming her, he had become a person of consequence, had all unwitting become their leader. He was—and he was not—pleased by it.

"*And* we must report this back to the others. This message about the vans and about the camp. We must pass it on." How could he have known that the news of the place was already known, not only as a rumor in a ghetto, but substantiated by one of the two escapees, passed on to the Polish underground, from there to the Polish government-in-exile. How could he have known that already by June of that year all the details were known even in London? All he knew was that the men agreed with him, nodding to congratulate themselves, though the boy Avenger was the slowest and Josef was not the only one to notice that his eyes were, the entire time, on the girl.

They moved through the forest only at night, and silently, the Avenger carrying the girl over the roughest parts to save her bare feet, allowing no one else to hoist her up. And she, in turn, seemed to want only his hand in hers, his arm about her waist, neither embarrassed that she wore nothing on her legs.

They let her bathe one night at a turning of the river, Oak and Ash and Birch and Rowan posted a half kilometer upstream; Holz-Wadel, Rebbe and Josef posted a half kilometer down. No one knew exactly where the Avenger stationed himself. In the morning, they could all see how springy and clean her red hair was, how shining her face, and that the scratches on her cheek and neck were already beginning to heal to three thin red lines. The roseate blooms from the gas poisoning had been replaced by a constant blush.

It took them three nights of travel to come around to the
first of the other partisan groups. Josef and Holz-Wadel
and the boy took Księżniczka to the leadership and told
them the story of what they had seen. The others thought
her name a code, like theirs, and approved of it. They
found her clothes: a peasant skirt, a shirt, boots only a size
too large which she stuffed with rags for the fit.

"We can send her on," a small man with round glasses
said to them.

Księżniczka clung to Avenger's arm. "I have nowhere
to go," she said, "no one who is wanting me." She looked
at Avenger but spoke to them all. "I do not want to be sent
on. Take me. Take me."

Josef remembered how he had used those exact words
when he had been driftwood, and his eyes burned with un-
shed tears. He put his arm around her and, inadvertantly
his hand touched the boy's. He forced himself not to
shrink from the contact. "We will take charge of her," he
said to the others. "We are her family now."

So she stayed and they found her a gun which she handled
badly, and a knife, which she used as if cutting apart a
chicken. But she was fearless nonetheless, and cheerful,
having no past to haunt her. Often when they were very
deep in the woods, she would sing quietly, for song lyrics,
at least, she could remember. One Josef thought particularly beautiful, a Yiddish lullabye. He learned it easily,
having a way with languages:

> *Shlof, zhe mire shoyn, Yankele....*

> *Sleep, Yankele, my darling little baby,*
> *Shut your big black eyes,*
> *A big boy with all his teeth–*
> *Should his mother still sing him lullabies?*

"You will have many big, beautiful, dark-eyed boys," Josef said to her one evening after she sang that song.

"And *you* will stay away from them," she answered back, but she touched his hand and smiled when she said it, to take away the sting. He wondered how she had known about him. He did not ask.

They had agreed not to go back to Chelmno because it was useless, after all, and too dangerous. Instead they joined the others in raids on tracks and depots once again, and they were over a year in the great track of the Polish forests, emerging every few weeks to blitz one small target or another, then fading back again through the trees and traveling miles away through the trackless woods. They lost very few fighters, except to influenza and occasional despair, though they sent many through the underground routes towards freedom.

But one day Holz-Wadel came to Josef privately.

"Rebbe and I," he began slowly, "we have been talking." That meant, Josef knew, that Rebbe had done the talking and Holz-Wadel the listening. But he said nothing. "We are thinking that this is not enough." He gestured around him, to the forest, but Josef knew he did not mean the trees. "We think that tracks and depots, depots and tracks are good, and of importance. But after what we saw in that field, this is nothing. We counted, you know. One year, one thousand a day. There can not be that many Jews in Poland."

Josef nodded, still silent.

"What do you plan to do about it?"

He had planned nothing, of course, but now his brain reeled with ideas. They could go to Vilna and help spirit children from the ghetto. They could join the underground of guardians who took people from Cracow, from Lodz. But a voice inside of him said, "We rescue one, they kill one thousand. Still—one is enough." He remembered the bitter taste of Księżniczka's mouth on his. And then, as if a fire had descended suddenly in his brain, he understood what Rebbe and Holz-Wadel wanted. And he understood why Henrik and his followers had cared more about mak-

ing a powerful story than life itself. He wondered only that
he had been so slow to learn.

He gathered them together under a large oak tree, away
from the other partisans. The oak was old and gnarled and
he leaned his back against it, borrowing from its strength.
The woodcutters stood shoulder to shoulder, clustered
around Holz-Wadel. Standing a bit apart was Rebbe, arms
folded over his massive chest. Księżniczka and Avenger
were arm in arm, her red hair now braided, reaching well
below her shoulders. He had the start of a fine beard, like
golden feathers, on his chin and cheeks.

Josef told them his plan. It was simple. It was direct. It
was deadly. He held out his hand. "Will you come?"

One by one by one they had nodded and taken his hand,
except for the boy who bit his lip. "First, there is something to be done," he said.

"What?" Josef asked, his voice smooth, but there was a
sudden chill in his chest and belly, as if announcing the
coming of bad news.

Księżniczka smiled shyly and taking the boy's hand,
she brought it up to her breast. "We wish to be married,"
she said. Then together they grasped Josef's hand.

Three days later, the marriage was held under a canopy of
sticks and leaves threaded through with vines. The woodcutters and Rebbe and Josef stood at the corners of the
chuppa to give the bride away. One of the partisans, a real
rabbi who had somehow managed to keep his white
fringed tallis through the months of living in the woods,
said the words over the couple as he remembered them,
for he had no prayer book. Those who had no head cov-
erings wore makeshift hats of wood. The few women con-
verted petticoats into headscarves. One even tatted a bridal
veil from the tassels of the rabbi's tallis.

The bride was given the marriage name of Eve. "Because," the rabbi said, "you are the first woman to be married here in the woods and because Księżniczka is not a

Jewish name." The groom offered his own real name: Aron Mandlestein.

There was no singing; it would have been too danger- ous. But when the rabbi pronounced them husband and wife in the sight of God and the groom kissed his bride shyly but with growing enthusiasm, a murmur ran around the ragtag forest congregation.

"Mazel tov," they all whispered, and Holz-Wadel ex- plained to Josef that it meant "good luck."

"Mazel tov," Josef whispered, too, though his eyes had begun to fog with tears and he turned away from the sight of all that happiness.

Then men with men and women with women—and the bride with the groom—they began to dance to no music at all around the clearing, the only sound their feet shuffling through the fallen leaves.

Josef stood apart, leaning against a tree, remembering Paris, Vienna, Berlin. Remembering Alan. Remembering life as it used to be and could never be again.

The nine of them left in the morning, tracking back to- wards Chelmno, returning out of life to death. It was late November 1943.

The woods were grey with the end of fall, Few birds sang. Then very early in the morning, the sky threatening rain, they came at last to the thinning-out of the forest less than a kilometer from the Chelmno fields. They did not know that in the year since they had been gone, the camp had been disbanded, then reinstated. That in the year since they had rescued Księżniczka from the pit, transports to Chelmno out of the Lodz ghetto had resumed at an accel- erated rate. That crematoria had been built in the fields to facilitate the problem of dealing with dead bodies as well as to aid in the reclamation of dental gold. That the num- bers of guards had multiplied.

And even if they had known, they would have come back.

They stopped by the Narew to wash, the men first and

then the girl, not so much to bathe but to prepare themselves for the coming fight. They dipped their hands into
the water and anointed their heads with it. Rebbe washed
his hands over and over and over again, muttering Hebrew
prayers. Then the men climbed up and turned away to let
Księżniczka take her turn.

She slid down the embankment and was just bending
over to wash her face when the machine guns split the
grey air with their chatter.

Holz-Wadel fell first, face down into the hard-packed
earth. Rebbe fell on top of him. Aron—Avenger—was
next and he made a funny sound as he went down, part
gasp, part cry. Ash and Rowan threw themselves to the
ground and tried to crawl towards him, but the bullets hit
them simultaneously, shattering both their heads so thor-
oughly, they no longer looked human.

Josef had been standing somewhat apart from them and
so had had a moment to try and flee to the Narew. He
never saw what happened to the rest. A bullet caught him
in the leg as he turned and he went down the embankment,
tumbling toward the river and Księżniczka who was still
bent over. He knocked them both into the cold water.

She screamed out Aron's name and tried to scramble up
to him, but Josef grabbed on to her and held her down,
partially to keep her from her death but also because at the
moment all thoughts escaped him and he was simply too
terrified to let go. The pull of the water caught them and
they floated entwined in one another's arms downstream,
chilled to the bone but otherwise unscathed.

After several meandering turns, they managed to haul
themselves out of the river and climb the embankment.
Księżniczka had to pull Josef after her, for his right shin
had been shattered. Alternately dragging him and cursing
him, she got him into the woods.

They clung together that night for warmth, not love, and
wept till morning for the others. But mostly for Aron.

She bound up Josef's leg and made a splint for it, using the knife she still had because it had been in a sheath held fast by her belt. Neither of them had managed to keep their guns.

Somehow they made it back through the woods over days or weeks, Josef was never to be sure. He was feverish much of the time. His memories of the trip back remained forever phantasmagoric. The one thing he could clearly recall was lying on his back, staring up through the canopy of trees, and thinking that the stars were falling until the first ones hit his face and he realized it was snow.

Two weeks after they found a group of partisans, the fever gone and his leg mending, but crookedly, Josef looked around for Księżniczka, but could not see her anywhere. As had become usual for him, he panicked when she was not close by, and he asked some of the women if they knew where she was. They pointed to one of the paths and he limped down it, looking for her.

She was kneeling in a small clearing, and at first he thought she was weeping. But she was not. She was vomiting quietly and efficiently into a small hole she had dug.

When he touched her shoulder, she turned around, simultaneously wiping her mouth with her sleeve.

"Are you ill?" he asked.

"I am with child," she said. "And I will not let it die."

So they forged papers for her in the name of Eva Potocki, and Josef gave her his stepfather's ring and his passport photograph in case she needed further corroboration. She would be a Polish princess traveling incognito, he told her.

She smiled. "And I shall never forget the dark prince who kissed me awake."

Since he never heard from her again, Josef convinced himself on good days that she had made it to America and

had come, once or twice, to Paris in the hopes of finding
him in a small cafe. But on the bad days, when his leg
ached with the wet and the cold, when he dreamed of
Aron dying with his mouth spewing blood in an arc like
a devil's rainbow, Josef was sure she was dead and the
baby with her.

HOME AGAIN

We say to fibbing children: "Don't tell fairy tales!" Yet children's fibs, like old wives' tales, tend to be over-generous with the truth rather than economical with it.

—Angela Carter: The Old Wives' Fairy Tale Book

Perhaps we are born knowing the tales for our grand-mothers and all their ancestral kin continually run in our blood repeating them endlessly, and the shock they give us when we first hear them is not of sur-prise but of recognition.

—P.L. Travers: About the Sleeping Beauty

CHAPTER

31

"Then he came at last to a tower room. It had a tin ceiling and a tin floor covered with latticework. In the middle of the room was a four-poster bed, fine damask curtains hanging from each corner. And on that bed lay the most beautiful young woman the prince had ever seen."

"How beautiful was she?" Shana asked. The picture she was drawing was of a princess who looked remarkably like Shana.

"More beautiful than the sun. More beautiful than the moon. With red hair as clean and shining as a river."

"Can she have blonde hair, Gemma?" Shana asked. She looked at her own drawing where the blonde princess lay, stiff as a piece of cordwood, on a large bed.

"If you like, my darling, your princess can be blonde."

"Can my princess have dark hair, Gemma?" asked Sylvia. Shana had taken the yellow crayon and refused to give it over.

"Dark indeed," said Gemma.

Little Becca was vigorously coloring her own picture. The red crayon firmly in her hand had already defined the princess's hair and body and, like the spilling of blood, had waterfalled onto the octagon that was the bed.

"And then what happened, Gemma?" Shana said. *"Tell the kissing part. I like the kissing part."*

"Me, too," added Sylvia.

Becca did not look up from her drawing, which was now completely red. It was as if she had not heard her sisters.

"He was so struck by the princess's beauty . . ." Gemma began.

"And her blonde hair," said Shana.

"Black," said Sylvia.

"Blonde," said Shana.

Their argument threatened to overcome the story's end.

"That he put his mouth on hers," whispered Becca to her reddened page. Then she stood and climbed onto her grandmother's lap, put her chubby little arms around her grandmother's neck, and kissed her right on the mouth, strawberry and peanut-butter sandwich and all. Gemma kissed her back as if the taste didn't matter.

CHAPTER

32

Becca and Magda had listened, almost without moving, to his recitation. His voice had a wonderful flow to it, and even the awful things he had to say were beautifully said. The fire had burned down twice and twice the plump housekeeper had come in, silently, to stoke it up again. She had brought in lunch as well, which they barely touched, and then later a tea which only Potocki had taken, more—Becca suspected—to soothe his throat from the telling than from any need to eat.

Becca had excused herself only once during the story, to find the bathroom, an elegant marble-floored powder room appointed in chintz and china. She had stayed in there longer than necessary, trying to take in all the details of the narration, trying to be thrilled with the idea of a grandfather who was a war hero, trying to understand that Gemma—her Gemma—had died and been resurrected by a kiss of life given by a man who had probably never kissed a woman before—or since. She thought suddenly, oddly, of Merlin Brooks telling her that she had no sense of the ironic. But the ironies in Potocki's story were too many and too overpowering. How could *anyone* have a sense of them?

Going back at last to the drawing room, she passed Magda but they did not speak. Indeed, except to refuse the food, neither of them had said a word the entire time. It was as if—Becca thought—they had been turned to stone by the telling.

"Wrong fairy tale," she whispered to herself, shaking her head.

When Potocki finished the story, his head dropped to his chest. He sat so long in that pose, Becca was suddenly afraid that he had passed out. Or died. She stood and went over to him, touching his hand tentatively.

He jerked awake, took one look at her, and whispered the name, "Księżniczka!" Then just as suddenly, he excused himself. "Oh, my dear, my dear, you *do* look so much like her. How could I have missed it?" He reached over to the table by his chair and rang the silver bell standing on it.

The housekeeper came back at once, flooding him with Polish.

He spoke back rapidly, then turned to Becca and Magda. "She worries so. And perhaps she is right to. I tire easily. But that is nothing. Just my age. The Potockis are a long-lived family. Unless they are cut down in their prime. She says that dinner has been sitting on the table for ten minutes already. She is very cross with us. Come." He had a little trouble getting out of the chair, but managed at last and, using his silver-headed walking stick, led them down the hall to the dining room where a feast waited.

Once they had been served, Magda nodded at Becca as if asking permission, then turned to their host. "I do not wish to be offensive, sir, you have been so very kind. But my friend Rebecca has come so very far to hear the truth."

"And you wonder, child, if I have told it, or if I have added something theatrical for the effect?"

"No, no, no," Becca said. "I think no such thing. Magda, how could you?"

"Dear child, she is right. I am, by my own admission,

a playwright and a liar. You gave me all the clues, you know: the ring, the town, the camp——even your grandmother's last name." He ticked them off on his fingers. "I *could* be making all this up. Yet another fairy tale."

Magda laughed. "*And* you like to play games."

"Games?" Becca asked.

Yes. When you are my age, there is little else to do. I have outlived all my friends—the ones who made it through the war. And all my desires. My dreams at night are not pleasant ones. One likes to remember being a hero, you know. I never got over his death."

"Whose death?" Becca asked. "Alan's?"

"Oh no," Magda said. "He was in love with Aron. With Avenger."

"Then it *is* true," Becca said, turning first to look at Magda, then at Potocki. "All of it?"

"Of course," Magda said. "He was the first to say her name—Księżniczka."

"In the forest?" Becca said, still looking puzzled.

"Last night, at the hotel," Magda said.

"I think . . ." Becca shook her head at Magda, "I think *you* like to play games, too."

Magda grinned. "It is not his age, you know; it is that we are Polish. If one does not play games, then there is too much to weep about. Is that not so, Josef Potocki?"

"That is so, lovely Magda." He kissed his hand at her theatrically. "But you asked about truth, young ones. 'What is truth?' said jesting Pilate; and would not stay for an answer."

"We stay," said Magda.

"We stayed," corrected Becca.

"And I told you more of the truth than I have ever told anyone. I gave Księżniczka the breath of life and she in turn gave it to you. How could I not tell you the truth of that?"

"You said you were not a hero, that there were no heroes," said Becca. "But I think you were a hero. And so was my Gemma."

He smiled. "Your own American writer Emerson said: 'The hero is not fed on sweets but daily his own heart he eats.' If that is a definition you can accept, then I will tell you I have dined long and hard on my own heart. And it is bitter."

Almost on cue the housekeeper brought in the dessert, a custard in individual dishes.

"But no more talk of heroism. Let us eat Madame Gdowski's crème caramel while it is still fresh. I taught it to her years ago and now that I can no longer cook it myself, she does the honors. It is—I must admit—better than mine."

As they were leaving the house, Becca took Potocki's hand. "I don't honestly think she remembered. Not you, not my grandfather, not any of it consciously. It had *all* become a fairy tale for her. She must have told us the story of Briar Rose a million times. But it was all there, buried."

"Just as well it was buried, my dear. I am glad she did not have my dreams." He bent over and kissed her hand. "Write to an old man now and then. I think I am your step-grandfather, in everything but name."

"Do you want your ring back?" Becca asked. "Or your photograph?"

"Oh no. I gave it to her as corroboration for her story. And now it belongs to you for yours." He smiled slowly. "Your grandfather was the real hero, you know. He dived into the pit of hell and brought her out of it alive. I can think of no one braver."

Magda stood on tiptoe and kissed him quickly on the cheek. "I can," she said. "Sometimes living takes more courage than dying."

And they left.

The next morning Becca drove them back to the field by the Narew. They got out, closed the doors quietly, and walked along the muddy road.

"Was it here, do you suppose?" Becca asked.

"Here—or close by."

They stared over the embankment down into the flat, grey water, then crossed the muddy road to stand in the field.

"Listen," Becca said.

Magda listened. "What is it?"

"Trees in the wind. The river going by. Birds."

"And you expected what? Screams? Cries? The chatter of machine guns?"

Becca shrugged. "I didn't expect it to be so . . . so quiet . . . so peaceful."

"A grave is always quiet. Always filled with peace."

Becca nodded.

"Unlike dreams," Magda said.

They got in the car and drove away.

They drove back to Warsaw without speaking, both lost in the story. The rest of the day in Auntie's apartment their conversations were full of the inconsequentials of planning the trip home.

"You found what you were looking for?" Auntie asked once. Only once.

"I found what I was looking for," Becca answered.

"She found more," Magda said.

"And less," Becca said. For the first time she realized that she did not really know how how Eve became Gitl, or if Gitl had been her grandmother's real name. And she realized, too, that she knew only that her grandfather's name had been Aron Mandlestein and that he had been a medical student. "And a hero." She hadn't meant to say it aloud.

"Poland is filled with heroes," Auntie Wanda said. "Six feet deep."

"Auntie, you read too many of the western books," Magda said, laughing.

That was the last they spoke of it.

* * *

While they got ready for bed, Becca turned suddenly to Magda. "Your Auntie is wrong, you know."

"Wrong? About what?"

"You snore," Becca said. "A little. I thought you should know."

"She snores, too," Magda said, an impish smile lighting her face. "That is why we do not share a room. But it is not polite saying this to strangers. Especially Americans, who expect everyone to sleep each in a single room. Yes?"

"My older sisters shared a room," Becca said. "And secrets. They were jealous that I had a room to myself, even if it was the smallest room in the house, not much bigger than a large closet."

"Smaller than this room?" Magda said, gesturing.

Becca smiled sheepishly. "A little."

Magda climbed into the bed and pulled the covers up to her chin. Hesitating a moment, Becca sat down on her bed. "I never got to know any of my sisters' secrets and thought I was missing something. And now I know my grandmother's—and I'm not sure I want to know. Should I tell them everything at home? Do you think Mr. Potocki would want me to? Is it better to let some things lie?"

"Let sleeping princesses lie?" Magda laughed. "We are all sleeping princesses some time. But it is better to be fully awake, don't you think?"

Becca considered for a moment. "Better for who?"

"For whom? I know this grammar. But I do not understand the question," Magda said. "Perhaps my English is not so good after all."

"Good grammar, bad English. Or rather, it may be your *American* that's lacking," Becca said.

"Americans do not want to be awake?"

"Oh," Becca said, "we like the truth all right. When it's tidy."

"Truth is never tidy. Only fairy tales. This is a very Polish notion. And you are Polish, you know."

"I know now," Becca said. "Good night, friend Magda."

"Good night, American princess." Magda turned over

and was soon asleep but Becca lay awake and thinking until nearly dawn.

The plane ride back was more than two hours late, but Becca slept almost the entire way. The Potocki ring nestled between her breasts on the gold chain Magda had insisted she buy. Even in her sleep her hand went to it.

Customs in New York was slow and she almost missed her connection to Bradley, but with some quick footwork she managed to make it just before they closed the doors on her flight.

She sank gratefully into her seat and got immediately into a deep conversation with the man across the aisle about late flights. It quickly turned into a discussion of her trip to Poland.

"Is it pretty?" he asked. "I've never been there."

"Not pretty," she said. "Not to me. But ... well ... haunting."

He nodded as if he understood. "Lots of old stories buried in those cities and towns, I bet."

She thought about the mud-colored street running past the ruins of the castle; about the old woman pointing them away from the men in the cloth caps who had threatened them. She thought about the burnished cheeks of the middle-aged priest and the way Potocki's hands shook on the silver-headed cane. She thought of the names of the camps as Potocki had spoken them—Sachenhausen, Dachau, Chelmno—like a horrible poem. She thought about a pit filled with corpses and a young hero bringing his bride-to-be up out of it into the clean air. She thought about the kiss of life. She thought about the silence of the field. She thought about what she would tell her family.

"Lots," she said, and ordered a club soda with a lime from the passing drink cart.

When she de-planed, she searched the gate area for her parents and then she searched baggage claim. She was surprised to see Stan walking towards her.

"Meeting someone?" she called out.

"You," he said, pushing his glasses back on his nose. "I asked your parents to let me pick you up. Your father said something about fast work. He's a funny man."

"He's a good man," Becca said. "And occasionally too funny for his own good."

Stan grinned. "And did you get your story? Find your castle? Meet your prince?"

Becca held out her suitcase to him and he took it easily. "Yes and yes and yes," she said. "I found out most of the story, but not all."

"Family stories are like that," he said suddenly seriously, leaning toward her.

"And the castle. It's called 'schloss.'"

"Really? Am I talking to a princess then?" He leaned even further into the story. "I'm not sure if the paper can afford a princess. Or even if it's politically correct to hire one."

"And I'm not sure . . ." Becca said slowly, working hard to keep her smile under control, "if I have any royal blood. But if you kiss me, I might just start to wake up. That's the way it goes in the fairy tale." She said it lightly so she could turn it into a joke if she had to.

He dropped the bag and stepped the rest of the way toward her. Taking her in his arms, he gave her a long and very satisfactory kiss.

When it stopped, she whispered, "It ends happily, you know, even though it's awfully sad along the way."

"Then let's start at the beginning," he said, picking the bag up again, and reaching for her hand. "With once upon a time. I'm not *that* fast a worker. We'll get to happily ever after eventually."

CHAPTER

33

"And as he did so, giving her breath for breath, she awoke saying 'I am alive, my dear prince. You have given me back the world.' After she was married, she had a baby girl, even more beautiful than she. And they lived happily ever after."

"The prince, too, Gemma?" asked Becca. "I don't think I was ever really clear on that point." She had come into the room just at the story's end, when Benjamin had taken his finger out of his mouth and offered it to his great-grandmother. Sarah was already fast asleep. She rarely made it all the way through the tale. She was only two.

"The prince, too," said Benjamin, offering his finger to Becca as well. She laughed and shook her head.

"I want to hear Gemma say it."

"You are a troublemaker. You always were," Gemma said, picking up the sleeping Sarah.

"No, Gemma, you have me mixed up with Sylvia. Or Shana. I'm the good sister, remember?"

"That's not what Mama says." Benjamin popped his finger back into his mouth.

Sleepily Sarah opened her eyes. "Seepin Boot?" she asked.

"Happily ever after," Gemma said firmly, "means exactly what it says." And one child in her arms, the other at her heels, she went directly up the stairs.

AUTHOR'S NOTE

We know this about Chelmno: that 320,000 people died there altogether, gassed in the vans. From February 22 to April 2, 1942, there were 34,073 exterminated. From May 4 to 15 another 11,680 people were gassed there. The Nazis were such exquisite record keepers. Numbers—not names.

The killings began in mid-January 1942 and, with several interruptions, ended January 17, 1945, when the guards slaughtered the remaining prisoners just ahead of the liberation by the Russian army. Two men—both part of the forced grave-digging detail—managed to escape, though shackled, in the early years. Two other men were miraculously alive in the camp at the war's end.

During the time that this book posits a rescue—June of 1942—there are no records of killings, which may mean that there were no actual deaths or more likely that those particular records have been lost.

The town of Chelmno exists. There may be a priest there, but I have never met him. There may be good people there. I have never heard them interviewed.

This is a book of fiction. All the characters are made up. Happy-ever-after is a fairy tale notion, not history. I know of no woman who escaped from Chelmno alive.

RECOMMENDED READING

FOR LOVERS OF FINE FAIRY TALES

FICTION AND POETRY

Katie Crackernuts, by Katherine Briggs
   A charming short novel retelling the Katie Crackernuts tale, by one of the world's foremost folklore authorities.

Beginning with O, by Olga Broumas
   Broumas's poetry makes use of many fairy tale motifs in this collection. (Available from The Yale University Press.)

The Sun, the Moon and the Stars, by Steven Brust
   A contemporary novel mixing ruminations on art and creation with a lively Hungarian fairy tale.

Possession, by A. S. Byatt
   A Booker Prize-winning novel that makes wonderful use of the Fairy Melusine legend.

Sleeping in Flames, by Jonathan Carroll
   Excellent, quirky dark fantasy using the Rumplestiltskin tale.

The Bloody Chamber, by Angela Carter
   A stunning collection of dark, sensual fairy tale retellings.

The Sleeping Beauty, by Hayden Carruth
   A poetry sequence using the Sleeping Beauty legend.

Beyond the Looking Glass, edited by Jonathan Cott
   A collection of Victorian fairy tale prose and poetry.

The Nightingale, by Kara Dalkey
   An evocative Oriental historical novel based on the Hans Christian Andersen story.

Provençal Tales, by Michael de Larrabetti
   Rich, subtle, adult fairy tales based on French legendry.

Jack the Giant-Killer and *Drink Down the Moon* by Charles de Lint
   Wonderful urban fantasy novels bringing "Jack" and magic to the streets of modern Canada.

Tam Lin, by Pamela Dean
   A lyrical novel setting the old Scottish faery story (and folk ballad) Tam Lin among theater majors on a midwestern college campus.

The King's Indian, by John Gardner
   A collection of peculiar and entertaining stories using fairy tale motifs.

Blood Pressure, by Sandra M. Gilbert
   A number of the poems in this powerful collection make use of fairy tale motifs.

The Seventh Swan, by Nicholas Stuart Gray
   An engaging Scottish novel that starts off where the "Seven Swans" fairy tale ends.

Fire and Hemlock, by Diana Wynne Jones
   A beautifully written, haunting novel that brings the Thomas the Rhymer and Tam Lin tales into modern-day England.

Thomas the Rhymer, by Ellen Kushner
   A sensuous and musical rendition of this old Scottish story and folk ballad.

Red as Blood, or Tales from the Sisters Grimmer, by Tanith Lee
   A striking and versatile collection of adult fairy tale re-tellings.

Beauty, by Robin McKinley
   Masterfully written, gentle and magical, this novel re-tells the story of Beauty and the Beast.

The Door in the Hedge, by Robin McKinley
   The Twelve Dancing Princesses and The Frog Prince retold in McKinley's gorgeous, clear prose, along with two original tales.

Disenchantments, edited by Wolfgang Mieder
   An excellent compilation of adult fairy tale poetry. (Available from the University Press of New England.)

Kindergarten, by Peter Rushford
   A contemporary British story beautifully wrapped around the Hansel and Gretel tale, highly recommended. (Available from David R. Godine, Publisher.)

Transformations, by Anne Sexton
   Sexton's brilliant collection of modern fairy tale poetry.

Trail of Stones, by Gwenn Strauss
   Evocative fairy tale poems, beautifully illustrated by Anthony Browne.

Swan's Wing, by Ursula Synge
  A lovely, magical fantasy novel using the Seven Swans fairy tale.

Beauty, by Sheri S. Tepper
  Dark fantasy incorporating several fairy tales from an original and iconoclastic writer.

Coachman Rat, by David Wilson
  Excellent dark fantasy retelling the story of Cinderella from the coachman's point of view.

Snow White and Rose Red, by Patricia C. Wrede
  A charming Elizabethan historical novel retelling this romantic Grimm's fairy tale.

Don't Bet on the Prince, edited by Jack Zipes
  A collection of contemporary feminist fairy tales compiled by a leading fairy tale scholar, containing prose and poetry by Angela Carter, Joanna Russ, Jane Yolen, Tanith Lee, Margaret Atwood, Olga Broumas and others.

A SAMPLING OF THE WORKS OF
MODERN-DAY FAIRY TALE CREATORS

The Faber Book of Modern Fairy Tales,
  edited by Sara and Stephen Corrin

Gudgekin the Thistle Girl and Other Tales,
  by John Gardner

Mainly by Moonlight, by Nicholas Stuart Gray

Collected Stories, by Richard Kennedy

Heart of Wood, by William Kotzwinkle

Fairy Tales, by Alison Uttley

Tales of Wonder, by Jane Yolen

The Power of Myth, by Joseph Campbell

The Erotic World of Faery, by Maureen Duffy

Women folk and Fairy Tales, by Susan Cooper
  (Essay in *The New York Times Book Review*, April 13,
  1975)

*Beauty and the Beast: Visions and Revisions of an Old
  Tale*, by Betsy Hearne. (Available from The University
of Chicago Press.)

Once Upon a Time, collected essays by Alison Lurie

*Here All Dwell Free: Stories to Heal the Wounded Femi-
  nine*, Gertrude Mueller Nelson examines Briar Rose and
The Handless Maiden.

What the Bee Knows, collected essays by P.L. Travers

Problems of the Feminine in Fairy Tales, by Marie-Louise
  von Franz, collected lectures originally presented at the
C.G. Jung Institute.

Touch Magic, collected essays by Jane Yolen

Fantasists on Fantasy, edited by Robert H. Boyer and
  Kenneth J. Zahorski—includes Tolkien's "On Fairy Stories," G.K. Chesterton's "Fairy Tales," and other essays.

A SHORT LIST OF RECOMMENDED
FAIRY TALE SOURCE COLLECTIONS

Old Wives' Fairy Tale Book, edited by Angela Carter

The Tales of Charles Perrault, translated by Angela Carter

Italian Folktales, translated by Italo Calvino

The Complete Hans Christian Andersen,
  edited by Lily Owens

*The Maid of the North: Feminist Folk Tales from Around
  the World*, edited by Ethel Johnston Phelps

Favorite Folk Tales from Around the World,
  edited by Jane Yolen

The Complete Brothers Grimm, edited by Jack Zipes
  For volumes of fairy tales from individual countries—
Russian fairy tales, French, African, Japanese, etc.—see
the excellent Pantheon Books Fairy Tale and Folklore Library.